"I feel what you feel, Paloma. Your thoughts are mine.

"In the darkest hours of the night, our dreams join and become as one."

That seemed to reach her. Her sobs calmed to ragged, shallow breaths; however, she continued to hold him tight.

"That's true, isn't it?" she whispered, shifting to gaze up at him. "I'd begun to wonder if I wasn't losing my mind."

"It's a strange phenomenon," Dunndrogo agreed.

She eased herself farther back to search his eyes. "How can this be?"

"I don't know." Ever so carefully, because he knew too well the strength of his touch and the sharpness of his claws, he wiped away the tears still slipping from beneath her long lashes. "I only know it is."

Dear Reader,

The New Year is here, and with it come new tales of dark and haunting love, tales written just for you by some of today's finest writers.

Start off the month with *Whispers in the Woods,* by bestselling author Helen R. Myers. I can guarantee that you've never met a hero quite like this before. His name is Dunndrogo, and he lives in the darkest depths of the woods, watching and waiting as Paloma St. John, a woman blessed with powers far beyond the ordinary, moves ever closer. And no one can predict what will happen when at last they meet.

Complete the month with *The Perfect Kiss,* by Amanda Stevens. Heroine Anya Valorian is as alluring as she seems—and far more dangerous. For inside her lurks a forbidden craving, a craving she must fight, lest she take the man she loves to an early grave. Will she fall victim to her own dark hunger, or will love's power prove the stronger?

Read them if you dare, then return next month for another taste of fated—if not fatal—love.

Yours,

Leslie J. Wainger
Senior Editor and Editorial Coordinator

Please address questions and book requests to:
Reader Service
U.S.: P.O. Box 1325, Buffalo, NY 14269
Canadian: P.O. Box 1050, Niagara Falls, Ont. L2E 7G7

HELEN R. MYERS

Whispers in the Woods

▼ SILHOUETTE® *Shadows*™

Published by Silhouette Books
America's Publisher of Contemporary Romance

SILHOUETTE BOOKS

ISBN 0-373-27023-2

WHISPERS IN THE WOODS

Books by Helen R. Myers

Silhouette Shadows

Night Mist #6
Whispers in the Woods #23

Silhouette Romance

Donovan's Mermaid #557
Someone To Watch Over Me #643
Confidentially Yours #677
Invitation to a Wedding #737
A Fine Arrangement #776
Through My Eyes #814
Three Little Chaperones #861
Forbidden Passion #908

Silhouette Desire

Partners for Life #370
Smooth Operator #454
That Fontaine Woman! #471
The Pirate O'Keefe #506
Kiss Me Kate #570
After You #599
When Gabriel Called #650
Navarrone #738
Jake #797

Silhouette Books

Silhouette Shadows Collection 1992
"Seawitch"

HELEN R. MYERS

satisfies her preference for a reclusive life-style by living deep in the Piney Woods of East Texas with her husband, Robert, and—because they were there first—the various species of four-legged and winged creatures that wander throughout their ranch. To write has been her lifelong dream, and to bring a slightly different flavor to each book is an ongoing ambition.

PROLOGUE

She'd never defied him before, not in the two years since her father's death, when he'd become her guardian. She'd never dared. But on her twelfth birthday, the opportunity presented itself when he went out unexpectantly. The instant he left to collect a special delivery package at the post office, Paloma St. John gave herself the gift of courage. All because she had to know what was going on downstairs in his private laboratory, specifically behind one particular door. A double-locked door.

The eerie sounds she sometimes heard from inside that room had become too much for her young mind to ignore. She wanted to offer help, if it was needed. But most important, she was hoping that her growing fears about her guardian's work, about Uncle Isaac himself, were unfounded.

From the beginning he'd discouraged her from coming downstairs. Children had no place in a scientist's laboratory, he'd scolded, the first time she'd ventured below to ask him for help with a homework assignment. That also had been the first time she'd heard the terrible sounds.

Uncle Isaac had explained it away as simply a few animals adjusting to their new environment. They weren't suffering, he'd insisted, nor would they. He did nothing like what the overzealous animal-protection groups were harping about at those school assemblies she'd discussed with him. After a few quick tests, none much more threatening than taking a blood sample, all the creatures would be presented to zoos across the country. But because they were *wild* animals, he'd refused to expose her to the possibility of being bitten. Not even for a quick peek.

At first she'd tried to give him the benefit of the doubt. After all, things *had* soon quieted down; however, in recent days the distressing noises had begun again, and this time there were louder cries, more desperate wails. And whether he wanted to admit it or not, her uncle was becoming more . . . tense. Strange.

She had to know why.

And today the door was unlocked.

Uncle Isaac was always the careful one, but apparently the news about the package had excited him and caused him to be forgetful. Paloma couldn't have been more grateful. As soon as he'd gone, she'd raced downstairs.

Now compressing her lips tightly to hold back a helpless cry of surprise or fear, she tightened her grip on the brass doorknob . . . turned . . . and pushed.

How easy. Too easy. Feeling her heartbeat all the way to the roots of her hair, she inched her head around the heavy steel door and looked into . . .

Darkness.

Then from inside came a sob, a whimper, a snarl. If it hadn't been for those sounds, she might have turned coward and pulled the door shut and run. She hated the darkness, feared it. Always had. For as long as she could remember. But pity, compassion, stopped her.

Did he keep them like this all the time? The very idea caused sweat to break out above her upper lip, and at her throat. Even so, she quickly reached up and flipped on the light switch to offer relief.

The room flooded with fluorescent brightness, stinging her eyes. But her discomfort was nothing compared to the shrieks that rose around the room. Blinking away the burning sensation, she looked... and wept.

I'm so sorry. So sorry. The silent cry ripped from her heart as she struggled to cope with this new truth.

The room was a prison for three orangutans and five chimpanzees. All were confined to individual cages, segregated cruelly so that no contact whatever was possible. The design of the compartments ensured that. Impossibly small to begin with, each was constructed of solid-steel sheet metal on three sides, restricting even visual contact. And it mattered, Paloma thought, aching for the miserable creatures. Damn him, it mattered!

She looked away, and immediately wished she hadn't.

On the opposite side of the room was a row of liquid-filled, storage containers where floating inside were— She clapped a hand to her mouth to stifle a scream.

The babies. Babies that had been too premature, too deformed to survive.

Her stomach lurched in revolt, her terror grew.

Why? Why was Uncle Isaac doing this? *How* could he do this? She'd believed he'd been carrying on her father's progress in healing, working to cure the dreaded cancers and other terrible diseases that had claimed so many lives from past generations and threatened so many in the future.

But this couldn't possibly be related to anything redeemable. This was hideous. This was a monster's den.

She spun away from the scene and found herself looking into the first cage, where an orangutan lay in a limp fetal position. It was reaching through the bars of its prison, reaching toward one of the containers. Staring in hopelessness. Too grief-struck to utter a sound. Or perhaps it had already retreated into the protection of madness.

Paloma tried, but couldn't hold back a sob.

With tears pouring down her cheeks, she stumbled toward the second cage. Its victimized inhabitant had a different hell to face. Unmistakably pregnant, the orangutan began rocking violently back and forth, her arms around her distended belly. Rocking, until she began slamming her head against the bars. Again and again, reopening old wounds on her forehead.

Helpless not to, Paloma reached out. *No! oh, stop. Please stop!*

Hair not speak.

She almost missed it. Like an afterthought, she grew aware of the words in her mind, yet couldn't actually swear she'd heard a voice. Wiping the flood of tears blinding her, Paloma shot a look over her shoulder, terrified that her uncle had come back sooner than anticipated.

But no one was there.

Of course no one was, she thought, disgusted with herself. If it had been Uncle Isaac, wouldn't she be running for her life?

Hair not speak, no. Harry say.

Paloma absently touched the hair that reached past her waist. *Hair?* She didn't know... *You mean me?*

"Paloma!"

This time there was no need guessing where *that* sound had come from. It was Uncle Isaac! But what was he doing back so soon? Oh, God, he was going to kill her for being down here!

She spun back toward the cages, and her gaze locked for a brief, panic-filled moment with the third orangutan. She'd never seen eyes so wise, so sad. So desperate.

No tell!

She didn't see his lips move, but his words permeated her consciousness as clearly as if he'd spoken out loud. She could tell he was the source from the way he stared, and from the intense way he gripped the bars of his cage.

No tell Hair speak. Hair be like Harry. No tell!

The sound of footsteps brought new screams from the other captives. It was a sound Paloma had heard dozens and dozens of times before. Only now they were more terrible, because now she understood the horror behind them.

And she understood what she had done.

What jeopardy she'd placed them in. Would *she* even survive her uncle's wrath?

More afraid than she'd ever been in her life, but knowing it was too late to run, Paloma watched him appear, fill the doorway.

"I knew it. I knew you couldn't be trusted," he ground out, advancing toward her.

She backed away, one step…three…five. Abruptly, she came up against hard, cold cinderblock. The sharp bite of the rough stones bit into her shoulder blades, and scraped at her skin. But it didn't matter. Nothing mattered except the sickening feeling of knowing she'd failed.

As her uncle reached for her, she shot a frantic look at the oldest orangutan. He shook his cage with new urgency.

No tell!

No, I promise. Never!

CHAPTER ONE

Nine Years Later

They were no longer alone. Paloma knew it even as the animals began showing their first signs of unrest.

She closed the bedtime storybook she'd been reading to the two chimpanzees and listened...not that she expected to hear anything. When she was outside the compound exploring or working in the woods, it took all her skill to pick up on the stealthy step of whoever, *whatever* watched them. It rarely cracked a twig or rustled leaves as it shifted a branch. What disturbed her most, though, was that this time it was exceedingly close. Closer than it had ever been before. With the iron gates locked, that meant only one thing: it must have scaled the eight-foot-tall stone wall and gained entry into the compound.

Picking up on her disquiet as much as the presence, Daisy and Ditto went quickly from uneasy to panicked. With high-pitched shrieks, they began shaking their heads frantically against the pillows of the cot they shared. Not wanting to let the intruder know just how upset they were, Paloma shot up from her cushion on the floor to smile down at them.

"No, hurt," she both said and signed, following the technique she was developing as part of their course of study. She drew the back of her hand from the crown of her head to her waist. That indicated "Hair," the name that the eldest member of their group had chosen for her years ago because he'd been fascinated with its length and lushness. Next she crossed her arms over her chest. "Hair hold Daisy and Ditto safe."

Brave words, she thought to herself, remembering how fragile good intentions had been at an earlier stage in her life, and how many lives her naiveté had cost.

Monster kill friends.

Belatedly, Paloma realized that Old Harry, the only orangutan to have survived the original group, was still awake and had picked up on her brooding.

No Monster here, she assured him, knowing who he was referring to. *No Monster close. Hair think truth.*

Who outside?

Who indeed? Paloma attempted a reassuring smile for the melancholy-prone primate, who, at nearly twenty-four was also the senior citizen of the family. *Lost friend maybe.* "Friend" was the term he'd taught her long ago to signify his fellow captives; an appellation that had touched her all the more when he'd awarded it to her.

He brightened. *Old Harry let lost friend in.*

Before she could stop him, he rolled himself backward off the worn green brocade armchair he'd laid claim to the day they'd arrived, and loped for the door. Paloma cast a worried glance across the open room toward the kitchen window where she most felt the presence, then dashed after him.

"No! Harry wait! Oh, blast..."

Although he was always welcome to follow any of the communication techniques she was studying with the group, she always tried to stick with mental telepathy as *their* method of communication. But this was hardly the time to worry about a slight infraction of the rules.

Grabbing his hand, she barely stopped him in time from unbolting the door. "No!"

Friend in come. Old Harry's saucer-round eyes reflected his hurt and indignation at being scolded.

What Hair speak? Not open door! She lifted her eyebrows in emphasis, ever aware that the rascal liked to challenge her for leadership whenever the mood struck.

Old home rule. New home safe.

Leave it to Old Harry to pull the rug out from under her, yet tug at her heartstrings all at the same time. Yes, that's exactly what she'd told him and the chimps, as she'd shepherded them from Byron's weekend farm in New Jersey—and away from renewed danger—to this lonely estate in northwest Maine.

She wished she could tell him that they were, indeed, as safe as she'd hoped to make them when she'd finally succeeded in freeing the survivors of her uncle's barbarous experiments from his lab almost a year ago. But maybe she'd again underestimated her uncle's determination to have his "property" back. Would things ever change?

Or maybe this was something else, something worse. But what could be worse?

If only the presence had made itself more clearly known before they'd settled in here. For the first few days she'd dismissed it as a particularly ill-humored black bear passing through the area. She was increasingly amazed at how over the past year she could pick up on more and more creatures' thoughts.

But it wasn't until their third week at the compound that she'd learned she'd underestimated things. Again. Badly.

Although she hadn't been as successful at picking up on its thoughts as she was beginning to be with some creatures in the woods, she'd surmised she wasn't the only one displeased over her misjudgment—and that the entity had an aura of incredible power.

She glanced down at Old Harry. *Safe when not open door.*

Pointing him in the opposite direction, she ordered him back into his chair. She could have chuckled over his miffed demeanor. When an orangutan decided to play thespian, there wasn't anyone more entertaining. But too concerned about what was happening outside, she hurried to the window.

In the mornings, the six-paned rectangle invited the late June sunlight to warm the four potted geraniums lining its ledge. Paloma had shoved the small kitchen table there so she could sit and sip an early cup of tea. There was no sunlight now, only the opaque black of a moonless, starless sky, and glass reflecting back her own solitary, pensive form.

What should she do? Her alternatives were limited by the life choices she'd made. A loathing for violence had canceled the option of carrying a firearm, even though her only friend and confidant, Byron—who'd been supportive in every other way—had called her a fool for that. All she had was the hiking stick she used when walking in the woods, the pocketknife on her belt, and the pitchfork in the barn. Not much of an arsenal. But then she'd been so sure that her only enemy would be her uncle, and that he would never think of looking for her here.

She directed her thoughts out into the night. *What do you want?*

Leave.

She gasped. Direct communication for the first time since this latest nightmare had begun! She didn't know whether to be terrified or thrilled.

Back on the fold-up camping cot, the chimps, although far behind Old Harry in championing telepathy, picked up the single, strong message. Scrambling to the center of the bed, they wrapped their arms around each other and resumed a soft keening.

Paloma commiserated with their fear. She, too, knew about suffering at the hands of a brutal dominant male, and that had been a male voice they'd just heard. But what species?

Who are you?

She received no answer. Had he gone? No, she thought; she could still feel him out there... somewhere. But encouraged by his tangible retreat, she edged nearer the window again and touched a hand to the trim of one pane. Concentrated.

We are friends.

The pulsating silence continued.

We mean no harm. Can you understand?

If he could, he didn't care to respond.

Paloma made a decision. She told herself she had no choice; she had to resolve this if they were to live here safely.

Glancing back at Old Harry and the chimps, she said and signed, "Hair go out. Friends stay."

Ditto shook her head vehemently, her sister covered her eyes with her hands, and Old Harry rolled off his chair again and squeezed himself between it and the wall. Not much more confident herself, Paloma snatched up a flashlight by the wood-burning stove and returned to the door.

She released the slide-bar lock and gripped the knob. With adrenalin surging, and excruciatingly aware of the weight of responsibility on her shoulders, she took a deep breath, and pulled.

A deafening roar cut through the warm night air like a knife.

Paloma slammed the door, secured the lock, and, terrified, threw her full weight against it. Then, yielding to quivering limbs, she slid to the floor.

Three pairs of eyes stared at her questioningly. She didn't have a clue as to what to tell them.

Dawn brought stiffness, a sore backside, and chills. Paloma lifted her head from the pillow of her knees, and saw Daisy and Ditto sitting on the arms of Old Harry's chair, meticulously grooming him. Such a scene of calm after a night of expectant terror.

As though sensing her attention, Old Harry glanced her way. *Monster gone.*

Thank you, Dr. Know-It-All.

He curled back his lips in a warning sneer. *No doctor! No doctor!*

Could she do nothing right? *Sorry. Bad word me speak.*

He nodded with enthusiasm. *Bad Hair.*

She let his naughtiness pass, since she felt she deserved worse. A fine guardian she'd proved to be, hunkered against the door too terrified to move.

With a sigh and groan for some newly discovered aches and pains, she shifted to her knees, then struggled to her feet. This morning she felt every minute of her twenty-one years, and then some. She probably looked twice that. More than coffee, she wanted a bucket of warm water so she could wash, and a brush for her hair. But those luxuries would have to wait. First she needed to check the house, and outside in the compound.

After a quick inspection of the lower floor, during which she blew out the oil lamps, she decided whatever had threatened them was gone. Returning to the front room, she unlocked the door.

Songbirds greeted her, along with sunshine and the promise of summer that underscored June's mild mornings. As welcome as all that was, she couldn't help but remember the roar that had haunted her for hours after she'd felt the presence retreat last night. Just thinking about it made goose bumps rise on her arms, and even her breasts.

What could have made such a bloodcurdling sound? She'd heard there were still a few bears up here, but those mammals were, if possible, less eager for contact with civilization than she and her fellow runaways were. Nor had she seen a sign of wolves. And there weren't supposed to be any big cats around, either.

Nevertheless, when she'd first stopped in town to refamiliarize herself with directions to the estate, she'd been warned about something strange and terrible stalking these woods. Supposedly even hunters had stopped coming to this area. What's more, rumor had it that her former guardian's tough, elderly sister had probably died of fright because of the creature.

How sad that, preoccupied with his own agenda, Isaac Tredway hadn't bothered taking time to attend Irene's funeral. With the arrangements planned long ago, he hadn't seen a need.

Unwanted, neglected, the estate had remained empty ever since. That's why Paloma saw it as the perfect hideout. Once she'd presented herself as Dr. Tredway's niece, no one had asked her for credentials or questioned her right to be there. To be sure, they doubted her sanity, but not her right.

The good news about the place was its size and the solid security walls. The fortress-like quality of them had been what convinced her that they could be safe here. But apparently she'd been wrong to believe the only threat she and her friends faced would be her former guardian.

Circling the two-story, white stone house, it disconcerted her to find no tracks. Whoever had come in had stayed on the grass or gravel. There were no marks on the wall, proving that whatever had scaled it had apparently done so without needing to claw or drag itself up and over.

Only as she paused near a huge knotty pine, whose heavy, high branches hung over a section of the wall, did she get a clue. That's how it must have gotten in, she thought with a shiver. Good grief. Either their intruder had the wings of a condor, or he could bench press more weight than she and her apes combined.

Or maybe he'd had a rope, she told herself as an afterthought. At any rate, she hoped he'd grown bored and moved to a different area now. She had firewood to collect for the stove, so they could boil the water from the old pump and stay warm at night. She also wanted to check on the wild blackberries due to ripen farther up along the stream. Anything was welcome that could help supply them with fresh vegetables and fruits to cut down on her trips to the village. One thing was certain: she couldn't allow herself, or the others, to become prisoners here. They'd struggled too long and hard for their freedom.

A few hours later, once everyone had been fed and she'd cleaned up, Paloma led her group into the woods. The sun broke through the canopy of pine and hardwood trees creating patterns of amber and emerald wherever they looked.

After a few minutes of intense wariness, she decided the intruder had, indeed, left the area and she allowed the chimps the freedom to explore and cavort. They raced for some vines and were soon up in the trees playing tag and filling the woods with their unique chatter and laughter.

Old Harry, of the insatiable appetite, inspected plants that might be edible, while urging Paloma to abandon wood collecting for berry picking. He was, she pointed out tolerantly, a bossy orangutan.

They all chipped in to get the wood collected, making several trips back and forth to the compound, until Paloma determined they had at least three days' worth stacked. Then she retrieved the basket they'd found in the house and set off for the stream.

Enchanted by the water, the chimps dipped their fingers in it, and floated leaves and flowers. Not only was play of any type still a luxury to them, but chimps usually had an aversion to water. That's why Paloma sat patiently on the bank, let them splash at each other, and her, and laughed outright when they did the latter with charming stealth. Old Harry, however, fancied finding himself a bed of lichen to lay on, and indulgently rubbed his always-sore feet.

When everyone tired of the playing and posturing, they hiked northward along the stream until the sky opened to a canopy of azure. A short distance beyond that, the berry brambles grew into a dense mass, creating a living maze that Paloma found as intriguing as it was eerie. Because it was only their second time up here, she cautioned the chimps about wandering out of sight. Old Harry needed no such warning, and she soon discovered the reason: her wiliest ape wanted to get first pick at the berries everyone else found.

Unfortunately, not much of the fruit had ripened yet. They collected what they could, and Old Harry struggled to restrain himself, though sporadically at best.

In the midst of scolding him for sneaking another mouthful, he dropped the basket and set off toward the compound. Paloma couldn't believe it. She didn't need him throwing a tantrum way out here.

Old Harry, stop!

Go home! The glance he gave her over his shoulder made it clear she had a full-fledged mutiny on her hands.

All go together. Friends careful.

Harry shook his head. *Go now. Monster come.*

Paloma experienced a moment's unease, then reminded herself that he might be pulling a fast one on her because of the scolding. "Harry, my boy, just because you didn't get your way, that's not an excuse to sulk or try to scare us."

Talk head talk. Old Harry speak. Monster come!

Even as he vanished behind the bend in the trail, she realized he'd been right. Suddenly she could sense the presence, too.

It had come back.

"Daisy, Ditto," she whispered, signaling the chimps to come to her. When they did as she'd directed, she urged them after the orangutan, ordering them not to stop or look back no matter what.

Her heart thudding, she then faced the direction where she felt the presence the strongest.

"Hello?" she called out, once again unable to determine who, or *what* she was dealing with. "Will you talk to me?"

Nothing happened. But the feeling of threat didn't lessen, either.

So much for trying to find out if it could speak. Obviously, like Harry, it preferred to communicate telepathically.

We mean no harm.

She wondered how basic she should keep her thoughts. Old Harry's limited vocabulary demanded she structure their conversations to an extremely simplistic format.

Like you. Want only home. Peace. Much room here. Much for all.

Once again there was only intimidating silence. Did she dare hope that meant it was willing to leave them alone?

Far behind her, she could hear the chimps' keening. She needed to get back to them. If anything happened to her, neither they nor Old Harry would survive out here on their own.

Had she made some pact with whatever was watching her? Would it attack if she turned and began walking away?

About to try a cautious retreat, she saw a movement in the thicket.

Her mouth had never felt so dry. Paloma swallowed hard and stepped toward it. This was important, too. For all of them. They needed to know what they were up against. They hadn't gone through all they had to settle for living in fear again.

She took another step, and another. When she was only a foot away, she could feel the presence on the other side of the bushes, feel its power. It filled her with as much awe as fear.

Would it attack? Would her death be quick and merciful or slow and terrible?

Ever so carefully, not noticing that her hand shook more than on the night she'd freed her uncle's laboratory animals, she reached toward the vine. Easy, she thought. *Easy.*

Suddenly, the whole bush shook and seemed to bow at her.

Choking on a scream, Paloma dropped to the ground and wrapped her arms around her head.

Less than a half hour later, he entered the mouth of the cave, and paused there to watch the woman sitting in the gold radiance of an oil lantern. She didn't acknowledge his presence, not even as he began descending the sloped path toward her. But when his great shadow fell over her, she lowered her mending onto her lap and sighed.

"What have you done?"

He didn't reply. He wasn't in a mood to explain himself.

"I heard the scream."

"She's not hurt, only frightened."

"You let her *see* you?"

His feral laughter filled the chamber. "Do you think she would have survived that?"

The woman made an aggrieved sound. "Don't punish yourself that way. It's just—" her voice took on an edge of panic "—I told you before, she had to be stopped before she settled into that place."

"I tried."

"So you tell me."

"She's brave."

"And *you're* intrigued."

"Enough!" The roar obliterated the muted thunder of the waterfall deep within the cave, and it sent the raven on a nearby ledge fleeing in fear.

Then silence settled again. Heavy. Awkward.

Weary, he turned away from her. "I'm sorry. You don't deserve this."

"Neither of us do," she replied, echoing the dispirited sigh he'd expelled. "Neither of us, my dear."

CHAPTER TWO

Even stillness could terrify. She'd learned the lesson ages ago. Although a full minute passed, and the worst didn't happen, Paloma stayed huddled on the ground, the silence of her surroundings vibrating in her ears so profoundly, it left a metallic taste in her mouth.

This had to be a miracle, she thought. Fortunately, she believed in miracles. She and her apes had survived too much not to.

But what had changed its mind?

Ever so slowly, she lowered her hands to the moss-covered ground. To balance herself. To feel. Was it still lurking in the brush? If so, what was it waiting for? Perhaps sporting with its prey was something it — *he?*—enjoyed. She'd read man wasn't the only predator to do that when he hunted, although the concept wasn't really understood yet by the experts, let alone her.

Go home.

Startled, Paloma glanced skyward. That hadn't come from nearby; nevertheless, she recognized the voice!

Where are you?

Slowly, she stood. Yes, she decided, she was alone. She could sense it now... and see the effects of that around her. The birds were returning to the brush, a rabbit, a family of squirrels. They remained cautious, but they were back.

How did you do that?

She considered herself little more than a novice at telepathy. Added to that, her nerves had yet to recover from their violent confrontation, so she didn't know if she could send her thoughts as well, as far as he seemed able to.

He? She frowned, realizing the pronoun shift felt right somehow, and not merely as a sexual connotation.

Go home, he'd said. She couldn't get over it. Gratitude flowed through her like warm summer rain.

Thank you.

Don't bother. Just go.

He'd heard her! She could barely contain her excitement. *You won't be sorry.*

She wanted him to know that. As she retrieved the basket of berries and started walking backward down the trail, she couldn't resist telling him again.

We'll do our best to honor your space. I promise.

It didn't matter that he didn't answer. She felt he'd heard her. Understood her. Despite the more complicated sentence structuring!

It was enough. More than enough.

Barely conscious of the ground beneath her feet, she spun around and raced back toward the compound. Farther down the trail, Daisy and Ditto called to her as they huddled under a fallen tree.

Her relief in finding them was as great as their jubilation over reuniting with her. Unsophisticated two-year-olds, the twins threw themselves at her, did acrobatics off whatever was available, and signed so rapidly she hadn't a hope of keeping up.

"Yes, yes, go home," she assured them, laughing because that's all she'd understood. Ultimately, however, she did pick up a bit more. "No, Hair not see Monster." It didn't seem fair to call him that under the circumstances. "Maybe not Monster. Maybe Friend after all."

Hand in hand, they hurried along the stream. To Paloma, the sky had never looked bluer. The birds had never sung sweeter. The sun had never blessed them with a more gentle warmth

At the compound they found Old Harry anxious, and eager to lock up. When he spotted them, he quickly assumed the role of patriarch.

Hair bad. Listen not.

Paloma knew he was right. More or less.

Next time, Old Harry talk— What was the best word to communicate what she meant? *—sooner.*

Hair kill Monster?

His mind bend disturbed her. *No, Harry! He not hurt Hair.*

What He?

Now there was the million-dollar question. *Hair no see what. No hear name.*

This proved very distressing to the orangutan. Much as it was with humans, what he couldn't see frightened him almost more than the threatening things that were visible.

Gesturing for her and the chimps to hurry inside the compound, he slammed the gate closed behind them. Paloma had to assist him in locking it, though. Despite all their practicing to master simple mechanics—like opening drawers and turning doorknobs—securing a lock on a gate remained a skill some weeks or months away.

Paloma was determined to teach them as much as she could. She wanted to ensure that if anything ever happened to her, they would at least have a chance at survival, until her only trusted friend, Dr. Byron Metcalf, could get them to someplace safe. Of course, the bonus to all those lessons was that she learned more than they did!

With the gate shut, the resilient chimps seemed ready to put their fear behind them. Paloma read their signals, and followed them to the storage shed on the right side of the house, where she kept their fresh food supply. She let them choose two bananas each for their lunch.

Old Harry curled his lip at the fruit and requested another egg, a treat he'd acquired a taste for since gaining his freedom. She told him that he'd already had his share of cholesterol for breakfast and would have to settle for either bananas, like the chimps, or a cup of nuts.

He chose the nuts, and carried the plastic container she'd marked with his name to the front stone porch. After a quick inspection, where she noted the depletion of their fresh stock, Paloma secured the shed, and brought up the rear. She'd made arrangements with the grocer in the village several miles away to buy a portion of his surplus every seven to ten days. By the look of things, another trip would soon be necessary. While in town, she thought she might phone Byron, and ask when he would be driving out for a visit.

She sat on the bottom step next to Old Harry, and brooded over what to tell Byron. She didn't have much progress to report on the primates' lessons; at least nothing that justified asking him to make the three-hour-plus drive from Portland, where he'd recently taken a job at a private behavioral science institute. As it was, she felt guilty for letting him convince her that he really needed someone to monitor a long-term study of primate learning abilities *outside* the institute's controlled environment. She was certain he'd only offered her the job so she wouldn't be dipping into her trust fund too often.

On the other hand, she wanted his input regarding what was going on around here. She needed to talk with *someone*, and hadn't Byron proved his trustworthiness by settling her and the apes at his New Jersey farmhouse, after knowing them only days following their escape from the lab?

But in all likelihood all he was going to say was, "I told you so"—and then try to get her out of here.

Resting her elbows on her knees, Paloma leaned her forehead against her clasped hands and admitted that once again she was in a situation well over her head. The story of her life. By now she should be getting used to it.

To identify a wrong—as she'd done with Isaac Tredway's hideous experiments—wasn't the most difficult thing in the world. Stopping that wrong, and replacing it with something good, was the challenge, and supposedly—per Byron—the first step toward wisdom.

In that case, she thought with increasing glumness, she should be brilliant. It had taken nine years to outwit her uncle. Nine years' worth of failed plans, of terror, and of overwhelming guilt as she was forced to wait for the perfect opportunity to escape. In the meantime, animal after animal she'd befriended had disappeared.

Now she'd let herself get caught in a dangerous situation outside the compound, when she should have ushered the apes back here to ensure their safety.

Maybe Byron had been right, maybe this place *was* all wrong for them. Never mind that she had a hunch it was the last place her uncle would look, if he chose to ignore the threatening note warning him of exposure that she'd left him after he'd tracked them down at the farm.

If the winter turned out rougher than normal, what then? Apes weren't meant to cope with blizzards. And most of the plant life was proving inadequate to a primate's needs. That meant more work for her than she'd been expecting.

She didn't mind the considerable expense of having to buy a greater portion of their food. Byron had helped her obtain full control of her trust fund when she'd turned twenty-one; between it and her project work for him, she could dismiss any financial concerns she might have for years to come.

But the time it took to replenish their supplies was another matter entirely. It meant leaving the animals unsupervised and unprotected for hours at a time, and that was concerning her *without* the intruder stalking them. And all that was just the tip of the proverbial iceberg.

What about the spartan life-style they were forced to lead out here? Every day she had to make certain she had sufficient firewood for the stove—and it was nearly summer! There was no electricity, inside plumbing, or refrigeration. That was all bearable now, but what would happen when it got cold?

What if the water pump froze? If it did, that would mean numerous treks back and forth to the stream that fed into the town lake.

Inevitable rationing. Countless challenges. Certain danger, now that they'd been told they were not welcome here.

But the bottom line was they were here because there had been nowhere else to go.

Paloma shifted her gaze to the sky, seeking peace if not strength there. What had happened to the warmth she'd felt only minutes ago? Why had fate made her life so different?

She'd never been what someone might call the average American girl. Not close to the image she'd eventually managed to see glorified in magazines— once she'd regained some of Isaac's trust to where he'd allowed her such luxuries. Because of her long confinement, crowds made her uncomfortable, and even one-on-one she had a tendency to be shy around people. For years, except for her uncle, her entire society had been composed of members of the animal world.

She'd never been on a date.

She didn't even know what it was like to watch a film in a movie theater, eat at a fast-food restaurant, or explore a shopping mall.

Isolated from the world, and forgotten by it, survival had demanded she learn to educate and entertain herself. She'd read virtually every book in Isaac's personal library. She could climb almost anything, and nearly as well as the apes could. She'd even discovered an aptitude for communicating on a different level that most humans couldn't fathom.

But she wasn't adequately trained to be responsible for these three lives, let alone her own. All she had was nerve.

Courage, Byron had called it.

As her thoughts drifted back to their experience in the woods, she rubbed her arms, thinking her friend had spoken more with his heart than his head. That was trouble of a whole other variety, and another reason why she kept telling herself not to lean too heavily on him.

Hair sad.

Old Harry's concerned observation forced her to reach for just one more ounce of inner strength. With a smile, she leaned over to touch her head to his shoulder. Apes had a need for physical reassurances, every bit as much as humans did.

Not sad. Thinking.

Old Harry think. He scratched the furrowed space between his great cheek pockets. His heavily lidded eyes watched her with an eerily Eastern wisdom. *Old Harry go say.*

Go where?

He pointed to the gate and the dirt trail leading toward the town of Vickery. Paloma felt a tug of compassion, aware that was his method for resolving any problem—simplistic deduction and immediate reaction. But Harry didn't understand that, at best, his method could only provide interim solutions. That much she understood regarding the differences between animal thinking and human logic.

Animals were content with the temporary—in this case to avoid danger—for all life existed to them on a tentative plain. Only man understood and planned for longevity.

Danger there, too. She shifted her palms upward and shrugged. *Here Old Harry, and Daisy, and Ditto run, play.*

No play. Monster.

There—she signaled toward the trail—*maybe more Monster.*

He took his time to brood over that. Finally he offered her a peanut from his cup. *Old Harry stay.*

Because Harry didn't share that often, Paloma thanked him with a pat on his hunched back before accepting his gift. Orangutans had a tendency to be solitary creatures, and since he was the only male, Old Harry also considered himself the dominant member of the group and above making too many gestures. As a result, Paloma looked upon this generosity as yet another link in their long relationship.

Inevitably, however, she refocused on the compound walls, and her thoughts drifted beyond them. Whatever were they dealing with out there?

No animal besides Old Harry had ever communicated with her so clearly. Some smaller species of creatures, a raccoon or a fox, could make her aware of its mood, for instance, but none had ever actually telegraphed the sound of words from its mind to hers. Because of that, and the mysterious stranger's obvious size, her vivid imagination kept wanting to give him a human face. But the growls from last night and those a while ago, made her realize how far off the mark she had to be.

Oh, she would be furious if someone was playing a nasty prank on her.

She hoped her parting words reconciled their situation somewhat. Because if they hadn't...

She couldn't allow herself to continue worrying. No matter what, she had to make things work out.

The day passed as the previous ones had, with an afternoon consumed by chores, exercise in the form of yard games, and lessons. By the time the sun set, Paloma was convinced that she'd at least succeeded in exhausting herself if not the others.

But as physically fatigued as she was, she discovered her mind refused to shut down. What she needed was some time alone, time to think without worrying that Old Harry would either accidentally or intentionally "eavesdrop."

First, though, she let the chimps unbraid her hair and take turns brushing it, a ritual they loved second only to trying on her clothes. Then she had to wait patiently as they groomed each other.

Finally, they settled down for the night on their cot. After assuring herself that Old Harry was fast asleep on his chair, she picked up her cardigan sweater from the foot of her own cot, and slipped outside to sit under the canopy of brilliant stars.

Sleep evaded him.

He rose from his bed of dried grass and silently left the cave, merging with the nearly moonless night like a shadow on black velvet. The wildness burned strong within him tonight. It made him restless. Tense.

He was hungry.

The need for flesh had been growing for days. Trying to resist it, he'd been sustaining himself on vegetation, roots. But the craving had become impossible to ignore. Overpowering. Far greater than his disgust for this loathesome part of his nature.

Tonight he had to yield to it. A life needed to be sacrificed in order for his own to continue. The urge to fill the darkness with his roar of challenge, and privilege . . . and, yes, regret, almost matched his hunger. But at least he won the battle over that.

It was not his way to torment his prey, despite the conflicting impulses that raged within his massive form. Will, he'd discovered through endless trials, could overcome instincts. To a degree. He might not be able to deny himself flesh, but he could claim it without yielding to *all* the rituals and viciousness passed down through his complex genes.

He lifted his head and drew in the scents of the night. No life-form ventured nearby. It came as no surprise. Most every living thing avoided him, even insects had been known to flee upon his approach.

It was just as well. Death didn't always come quietly. If he could accomplish his task in solitude and without upsetting every other life-form within earshot, it left that much less guilt for him to deal with.

He glanced over his shoulder into the cave and listened. She slept. It was safe for him to leave.

But what of the other?

He looked toward where the sun had set. Over the tops of the trees, the sky had yielded its orange fire to the dense cover of indigo . . . and little else. No lights from her house relieved the darkness. As usual. Except for those first few nights when she'd moved in and had burned the litter that had accumulated in the neglected place, she had been living in that fortress of a house as quietly, as frugally as they lived in their cave. But when the wind was right, he could smell the smoke from her stove.

For her sake, he hoped she and her creatures were asleep by now. Heaven knew she should be, considering the fright he'd given her today. Then again, if she did hear the sounds of his hunt, perhaps that would convince her to leave these woods once and for all.

A low, involuntary growl rose in his throat. The craving was intensifying.

He descended the sharp rocks. After leaping the last few yards to the mulch-covered earth, he sprinted off into the woods.

The chase reduced him to a creature of sensation. He relished hearing the ground rumble under his considerable weight like distant thunder, enjoyed watching limbs recoil from the sheer force and momentum of his power, thrilled feeling the wind glide across his face and body like the caresses he'd long denied himself, and those he would never know.

It pleased him to know that, at any instant, he could stop and become as still as stone. Sometimes he ran for miles, especially when there were supplies to replace. Then it was imperative that he get in and get out of the village in the dead of night without being noticed. And no one did, except for an occasional canine or feline. Sometimes they howled or whined, but most of the time they simply ran in terror.

Tonight his hunt didn't take him that far. He'd gone only a mile or so along the stream, when he came upon his hapless victim. Too involved in quenching its thirst at the melodious stream, it sat oblivious to impending danger. Fortunately, or unfortunately, it was perfect for him; the smallest life-form available that could satisfy his hunger.

Spotting him, its stress was so great, it didn't even try to run. It just sat there waiting for the inevitable.

Paloma had barely stepped off the porch when she heard the wail. Brief, but high-pitched, it sounded like a child's cry, and stopped her in her tracks.

Dear God, what had that been?

She wrapped her arms around herself against the unexpected, inner chill that was so much more depleting than the cool night air. The silence that followed brought tears welling in her eyes because subconsciously she knew the answer to her own question.

She understood the cycles of nature, the cost of survival. But she loved animals, so much so that she'd found it necessary to become a vegetarian.

Slowly, cautiously, she approached the front gates and stood with her head pressed against the bars looking out into the black abyss. *Go softly, gentle soul,* she prayed, feeling diminished by the loss that was almost a physical presence to her.

Oh, yes, she was convinced animals had souls. She'd held too many of them in her arms during their last moments not to believe. She'd seen the look of awareness in their eyes, and had heard the whisper of their last breaths. She'd experienced the mystical change that occurred right afterward, the phenomenon that took only a heartbeat, as the spirit withdrew from the body.

At the same time, she couldn't despise what had taken the life out there. Poor creature...it had no control over what evolution had planned for it. All she hoped was that the deed be performed with the full skill of its predator's breeding, and so be mercifully fast.

About to turn back to the house, she hesitated, her gaze locking on a shadow separating itself from the others. Just as quickly she told herself she'd been wrong.

What she'd thought she'd seen had been so big, surely her eyes were playing tricks on her. Besides, she hadn't really noticed a form, just a shifting of darkness.

But a moment later, she realized she hadn't been wrong. She knew she was being watched.

She could barely breathe.

"Is it you?" she whispered through the bars.

She waited, expectant. His reticence made her all the more certain she'd been right in her hunch.

I can feel you, you know. You're toward...my left, near the big spruce that looks as though it was hit by lightning a few years ago.

She felt his surprise like a shifting of the air. Then, ever so faintly a twig cracked.

"Don't go!" Encouraged that he had understood her, she couldn't hold back the outburst.

"I—" *I'm lonely tonight. My friends are asleep and I've no one to talk to. You seem... Well, despite being afraid of you, you seem very easy to communicate with.*

Confusion and doubt seeped out of the darkness, slow to filter into her mind, and then only in fragments. At first.

You don't have to come closer. Just stay with me for a minute or two. There was a cry in the woods a short while ago—you must have heard it. It's making me feel as though the stars have never seemed more far away. Do you understand what I mean?

Maybe she'd been wrong, after all. Or else she was asking for too human an emotion from him? Her head throbbed as she felt herself thrust back into her initial confusion about what she was dealing with. And if this was an animal, exactly what it felt spiritually remained mostly a mystery to her.

But sensing a conscious withdrawal of the presence, she was more determined than ever to get some response.

Look, I'll step behind the wall, so you don't have to feel the violation of my eyes. Would that make you feel better?

She did just that, moving quietly, but not too quickly in an effort not to startle him. She thought it might help, since many creatures found direct eye contact objectionable, even a sign of aggression. But again she had one small problem between her logic and instincts—she didn't feel as though she was speaking to something like Old Harry or the chimps.

There. Is that better?

You won't leave, will you?

The filtering of his voice into her mind drew a bemused, relieved smile from her. It felt so strange and yet wonderful. Much more physical than any connection she'd ever experienced before.

She began warmly, *No, don't worry, I'll—* Then it came to her that he hadn't meant "leaving" as in going back into the house at all. Her pleasure turned to disappointment.

No, I'm not leaving. Please, understand. We must stay here. If we left the woods, we would be in danger. We can't live where others do. Can you understand that?

His response was slow in coming, and reluctant. *Yes. But you're no safer here. I, too, could harm you.*

You had the opportunity today, and didn't use it.

Take nothing for granted.

What changed your mind?

He didn't reply, and she couldn't read his thoughts nearly as well as he could obviously read hers. But after several seconds, she heard a weary sigh from the other side of the wall.

Suddenly, she felt ashamed. *Never mind. The gift is in knowing you did.*

Once again silence stretched between them. Then with undeniable reluctance he opened his thoughts to her.

You disturb me.

Disturb?

I don't understand you.

Paloma turned to face the barrier between them, and laid her hand flat against the cool stone. *Do you want to?*

Again there was confusion. Conflicting emotion.

You're not like others.

It wasn't quite the answer she'd been expecting. Once again she felt off balance, not knowing whether to be disappointed or flattered. *I imagine not. I've had what you would call an unusual life.*

The life you live here is not normal for someone like you.

True, but it's necessary because we're free here.

Not before?

No. We were like . . . prisoners. Captives.

Prisoners are kept behind bars. Captives in cages.

She felt the tightening in her chest and couldn't attempt a response for a moment because she had to concentrate on forcing air into her lungs. She still had that reaction sometimes, when memories of the past grew too vivid.

It was his curiosity, his willingness to learn that gave her the strength to go on.

The others always lived in cages, and . . . sometimes when I was bad, I, too, was kept in a cage.

A feral growl, soft, but unmistakable came from the opposite side of the wall. It startled Paloma enough to get her mind off herself. Who was this strange being that he should protest like a beast, and yet make her feel his outrage on her behalf?

She had to know. *You understand cages?*

There are those who would put me in one—or worse—if they could.

Are you the—the one the townspeople speak about?

When she'd told the grocer where she would be living, he'd become extremely upset and had asked her if she knew what she was doing. Of course, she hadn't wanted to confide any more about herself than necessary. But even so he'd been determined to frighten her with tales about Vickery's very own monster.

Rumor had it Irene Sims had died of fright after seeing it. As a girl, Paloma had met Isaac's widowed sister, and thought it highly unlikely that the woman could be afraid of anything. Even her brother.

Realizing he hadn't answered her question, Paloma whispered, "Are you still there?"

What did you do that made you bad?

Maybe he couldn't speak in the way she could, but he clearly had a strong, focused intellect. It allowed Paloma to overcome the pain and terror of her memories and stay with his line of focus.

I tried to free my friends from their cages. I tried to save others from being... used.

Her reply had a significant impact on the stress level between them. She picked that up clearly, and wished she understood more about what was going on in his mind.

Explain used.

They'd been chosen for— Even now it was difficult for her to face it *—genetic research.*

A terrible groan rose from the other side of the wall. Then Paloma heard the sound of scrapes, like nails cutting into stone.

She winced. "Are you all right? Let me come—"

Stay!

Already shifting sideways and reaching between the bars, she jerked back her hand and pressed flat back against the wall. His fury was every bit as paralyzing as it had been this afternoon.

Pressing her hands to ease her thudding heart, she tried to think of what she'd done wrong to set him off like this. He quickly stopped her.

It's not you, it's me.

She exhaled a shaky breath. *I'm sorry, I don't understand.*

It doesn't matter. And don't open the gate.

Why not?

Don't question me!

Paloma rubbed her damp palms against her jeans. *Why are you trying to terrorize me again?*

Think what you will, but stay where you are.

All right, she thought, she would because she yearned to recapture the more peaceable mood that had existed between them. But it didn't slip by her that the woods had grown strangely quiet since his arrival. Did every living creature fear him?

Now you're beginning to understand.

His mind, his power mesmerized her. *You don't want me to see you.*

No.

Is it because you've been...maimed? I wouldn't be repulsed.

You don't know what you would feel. You're a foolish young girl who takes too many risks. You know nothing about what you're dealing with.

Hurt sliced at her heart. She didn't deserve that from him.

I could destroy you with a sweep of my hand.

But you wouldn't. No matter what, she would hold to that thought.

These are my woods you're trespassing in. Don't be too sure. Did you hear that cry a while ago? I know you did. I felt you as clearly as though you stood next to me. Do you know what I did to that small creature?

CHAPTER THREE

Don't! Paloma couldn't bear his cruelty.

Will you do as I say?

I told you, I can't leave. We can't.

Another snarl rose from behind the wall, and he struck the solid stone with a force that shook it. *Then let it be on your head. In the future, you stay out of mine!*

He'd demanded the impossible. How could she forget him, when she had to structure her entire existence around trying to pacify him?

For the next few days Paloma did her best. She confined herself and her three housemates to the compound as much as possible, thrusting them all into a schedule that was both mentally and physically demanding. But there was no shutting off her mind completely to her curiosity about the reticent prowler who roamed the woods.

The weather grew warmer, although it remained unpredictable, even for Maine. On the day when she knew she could no longer hold off driving into town for supplies, Paloma considered the gray clouds moving in from the west with trepidation.

This was what she got for procrastinating. Of course, she hadn't been doing that; she'd been waiting until she felt confident enough to leave the compound for an hour or two. Could she get through her errands in time to return before the rains came? Spring and summer storms were tricky, no matter where one lived, and she didn't want to leave the chimps and Old Harry alone any longer than necessary.

It couldn't matter. Those blessed supplies were vital. And there was that phone call to make to Byron.

"I won't be long," she said, when she finally finished with her preparations and was ready to go. She signed to Daisy and Ditto who'd been told to stay indoors with their toys and play until her return. "Promise to be good and listen to Old Harry."

Daisy covered her eyes and stuck out her tongue, letting it be known what she thought about the idea. But wide-eyed Ditto nodded, while rocking back and forth with her stuffed bear. Paloma hoped the more docile chimp would prove a calming influence on her sister. Sometimes Daisy and Old Harry could squabble like an old married couple.

The orangutan sprawled across his chair and pouted. He'd wanted to go along. "Please, understand," she told him. "If I took you with me, you'd attract too much attention. Too many questions. Remember how people stared when we came to town that first time? And then they'd only gotten a glimpse of you." He'd become belligerent as a result of the blatant staring.

Talk head. Old Harry good not hear.

He was punishing her, of course, because she knew full well that through the years he'd learned to understand at least the underlying tone of her spoken words, not to mention Isaac's grim threats. But Paloma had no time for a contest of wills, nor did she need a rebel. She wanted an ally.

Old Harry help Hair. Old Harry wise. Watch friends. Be good. Hair get food quick. Back soon.

Old Harry pretty get?

"Pretty" had become his term for anything flashy, whether it was a child's pinwheel, a brightly colored ball, or a crepe-paper party horn. She had no idea where he'd developed the fascination for such things, just as she wasn't certain about how he'd developed his telepathic skills. She did, however, know that his eye for glitter had been enhanced after they'd watched their first New Year's Day parade on the television at Byron's farm. After his and the girls' initial terror, the trio had become fascinated with the pageantry and animation of the various floats.

Hair look for pretty. Promise stay inside? Keep door locked?

Once the orangutan nodded, she gave him a hug, as she'd done to the others. Then she hurried out to the secondhand van Byron had helped her purchase.

It took another few minutes for her to let herself out the gate. As she went to lock it behind herself, her gaze was drawn to the scratches on the outside wall—something that was fast becoming a habit, the same way it was becoming automatic to check the doors and windows every night.

Running two thirds of the way down, the marks were clawlike incisions, except that no fingernail should have been capable of cutting into such a tough surface, certainly not that deeply. A troubling thought. But not as disturbing as the blood had been.

The first morning she'd seen the red marks on the wall, she'd run for a pail and brush. With a strong detergent added to cold water, she'd begun scrubbing away at the gruesome sight. She'd worked desperately, until all traces of the stain were gone. Maybe she'd been trying to convince herself that if she could remove all evidence of it, she wouldn't have to deal with what it meant . . . or wonder whose blood it was.

Fighting off another shiver, she locked the gates behind her. She would take no chances. On either side, she thought, seeing all three of her animal friends watching her from the kitchen window. With a sigh and a wave, she quickly climbed back into her van and drove off.

The cloudy skies, plus the already dense veil of trees, made the trip to town a darker journey than usual. Paloma negotiated the narrow trail with great caution. Not only was she a relatively new driver, it also concerned her that at any second some creature might dart out in front of her van. She could never forget that one of the first discoveries she'd made after gaining her freedom was the appalling number of animals that got struck on a daily basis by moving vehicles.

The trip, however, passed uneventfully. Arriving in town, she went directly to the pay phone by the gas station to call Byron. She heard the first rumble of thunder as she dialed, and it began to drizzle as the connection was made.

"Byron?" Paloma stepped deeper into the glass booth, despite the claustrophobia that made her want to stand as far away from it as the cord would allow.

"Paloma! Are you all right?"

She smiled, wryly. He always began their conversations this way, expecting the worst. Apparently, she didn't inspire confidence in anyone.

"Fine. About to get soaked, though, so I'd better keep this short."

"How's it going over there? Settling in?"

"Progress is slow, but we're getting there. It's different," she added, the confession slipping from her lips before she could realize what she was saying.

"Too scary?"

That forced her to harness her feelings faster than anything. "Compared to what?" she asked quietly. No matter what life presented, she would never forget where she'd come from and what she'd seen. She could survive anything now, and she mustn't forget that.

Byron cleared his throat. "You've got a point there. But for a minute you sounded...well, you can't blame a guy for worrying, can you?"

She touched the mouthpiece, as she would have his cheek if they'd been standing face-to-face. "I appreciate the concern."

How she wished she could be more adept at men-and-women things. At thirty, Byron was long past deserving of having someone in his life who made him happy. From the moment they'd first met, when he'd literally bumped into her at the produce stand where she'd been buying some fruit for the apes, he'd been the kindest, most considerate person she'd met. What's more, the quietly handsome scientist had made no secret about how quickly he'd developed special feelings for her. Heaven knows she owed him for taking so many risks for them.

But no matter how much she tried, she couldn't make affection and gratitude turn into anything more.

"How's the new job?" she asked, forcing more enthusiasm into her voice.

"Terrific. Terrifying. Challenging."

"Everything you like." Paloma smiled to herself, aware he was being more modest than honest.

"We make a team, don't we?"

She sensed more than understood what he meant, and wondering how to answer, she once again felt frustrated by her inexperience in this arena. "You're the natural, Byron. I'm more like an innocent bystander who got tugged into the rapids and still hasn't mastered dog paddling . . . Byron?"

She'd meant her analogy to be a joke. Instead there was a long silence on the line. Finally, he muttered, "I knew this was too good to be true. What's wrong?"

No doubt about it, she was better at mothering animals than dealing with the opposite sex. She caught a glimpse of her reflection in the telephone's chipped and rusting chrome. A pale, makeup-free face that was mostly eyes, made darker by a rope of black, black hair. No wonder people always treated her as though she was half her age.

There was no denying it, she was simply a skinny misfit. It didn't matter that she hadn't gotten around to even identifying if she had any physical assets to work with because she was still too busy fighting for survival. She was emotionally inept at being a woman.

In other words, Byron had seen through the reason for her call, after having hoped she'd phoned because she'd been missing him. Suddenly it became imperative that she not blurt out her concerns regarding their strange visitor. No, she mustn't. Not only would he be concerned, he would drop everything, risk anything, to drive directly out to the estate.

She had no right to do that to him, especially not when he'd just taken on the job of a lifetime. A position that would someday prove animals such as Old Harry and her chimps were not so different from humans, and that it was an atrocity to use them as if they were senseless test tubes.

"Nothing's wrong," she said firmly. "It must be this gray weather you're hearing in my voice."

That had him thinking for a moment, and she could almost hear the gears in his mind turning as he deliberated whether to buy into that explanation or not. "Okay," he murmured at last. "How's the gang?"

Paloma could have sighed with relief. "Oh, Byron, they're adjusting beautifully," she gushed brightly. "They love the wooden-block puzzles you gave them, and the bedtime stories are a great hit. And you were right about Ditto taking comfort with that stuffed bear. She doesn't have nearly as many nightmares as she did in the beginning."

"It sounds as though things are perfect."

Well, she *would* love to have a hot bath without having to tote in water from outside and heat it on the stove first. It also would be heaven if they had electricity, so they could have a refrigerator....

"We're adjusting a bit better every day." There, she thought, satisfied she was more in control. Maybe now she could get some information without upsetting him more than she already had. "Er, the reason I called is that I wanted to ask you something about my telepathic abilities."

"You haven't noticed a decrease, have you?"

She could sense the alarm in his voice. As wonderful as he'd been to them, Byron was first and foremost a man of science. Matters of the heart aside, her special skills had been the strongest catalyst prompting his decision to stick his neck out for them. He had a personal interest in expanding the communication skills between man and the creatures with whom he shared the planet.

"No, actually..." Be careful, she warned herself. "I was wondering if perhaps they were getting more developed. I mean, could I be fabricating that in my own mind just because I want to?"

"You have to give me a bit more to work with, Paloma."

"Well, sometimes I think I'm receiving more complete sentences. How's that?"

"Interesting. Great. You'll remember that from the beginning I thought you might, once you settled down in a relaxed environment. Do you recall when I said that studies suggested telepathy fluctuates with, and was closely tied to, the emotions?"

"Yes, I remember." He'd explained how the deeper the emotional involvement between two subjects, the more profound the connection.

"In other words, this is exactly what we've been waiting for. Are you keeping thorough journal documentation?"

She chewed on her lower lip. Document *what*? She didn't even know who her subject was yet. "Um, you know, Byron, it only just started."

Byron all but groaned her name. "I know how suspicious you are of the scientific community, but you have to try not to judge everyone by your uncle's actions."

"He's *not* my uncle," she muttered, feeling as though she was losing control of the conversation again. "And you know that except for you and the few others you've assured me are out there, I think the scientific community can take the next shuttle to Saturn."

"Paloma, honey, all I'm saying is that if we're to turn your bad experiences into something good, as well as honor your work with the apes, your records will have to be complete and accurate."

Paloma rubbed her palm against her forehead. "I understand, Byron, really I do. And I want to pay you back for all you've done for us."

"Hold it right there."

She could hear an almost pained note in his voice, and knew she'd worked too hard this time at keeping him at arm's length. Now she'd hurt him. Oh, God, what a mess she was making of all this.

"What did I say about gratitude between friends?" he asked too quietly.

After his first overture, and her gentle rejection, she'd been overwhelmed with guilt. For days thereafter she'd felt a compulsive need to say "thank you" for the slightest kindness he'd shown her, until he'd exploded.

"'Gratitude is a dry well that only friendship can fill,'" she recited.

Byron sighed. "I wish you'd stop forgetting that."

"It's your own fault," she tried to tease. "You're just too good to me. To us. You're not supposed to be real."

"Trust me, I am. And I've got the feet of clay to prove it. So..." he added with forced cheerfulness "...how's Harry taking this new breakthrough with you?"

Paloma frowned at the intensifying rain, realizing she was going to have to confide in him, after all. "It's, er, not Old Harry."

"You can't mean it's one of the girls? Why that's fantastic! It's Ditto, isn't it? You know, I had a hunch about this, and I bet it'll only be a matter of time before Daisy starts."

"It's not Daisy or Ditto, either."

Byron's hesitation spoke volumes. "Then who are you having this expanded communication with, Paloma?"

"I don't know."

"What do you mean, you don't know? There has to be something, some*one* around."

"There is. I've heard him outside the compound, in the woods, but I haven't seen him yet."

"What makes you so certain this contact is a 'he?'"

"His authority, his phrasing." Paloma gestured helplessly. "I don't know how to explain it, Byron, I hear an intense masculine voice when he communicates with me."

"I don't like this at all," he muttered. "It sounds to me as though you have someone stalking you from town. I want you to pay a visit to the police right after you hang up."

"Absolutely not."

"Why?"

The phone booth had a leak. Paloma pressed against one of the glass walls just as a louder peal of thunder sounded. "Because the first thing they would say is that I have no business being out there by myself."

"Good. It's about time you heard that from someone besides me!" he shot back.

This was getting them nowhere, and the weather was getting worse every second. A bigger flash of lightning had Paloma ducking deeper into her sweatshirt. "What if it's not a person, Byron? What if it's a bear or something?"

"A bear? Communicating in more complete sentences?"

"Okay, I know, I know." Actually, she didn't know what she meant anymore. All she'd wanted was some input. She hadn't expected to be treated as though she was losing her mind. Wasn't she the one who'd survived years of confinement and intimidation, and had saved the lives of those who'd been dealt far worse?

"I don't care that it sounds farfetched. The point is that no one's moved back out there since Irene died. From everything I understand, the timber companies finished harvesting the tree stock in the area and they moved on. That was almost eleven years ago. The one time my—Isaac took me there."

"Fine. It's not a local person. Then consider this... from what I saw during my brief inspection, you're near some steeper terrain. For all you know, you might have a hermit homesteading in a cave or something. In this day and age, there's everything from survivalists to political extremists hiding out in remote areas, pretending they're a cross between Thoreau and Daniel Boone, or who knows what."

''But you don't think it could be an animal?'' she asked, not willing to tell him the rest—like how the villagers spoke of a wild beast in the woods that had occasionally attacked their domestic stock, and had even invaded their businesses on occasion.

''What I think,'' he said grimly, ''is that you might have a modern-day Jack the Ripper out there, and you'd make me feel a heckuva lot better if you'd stop sounding as though you're about to adopt another stray into your menagerie!''

Was that what she was doing? Perhaps she was, but only because she had a feeling that *stray* seemed as soul-tortured as any being she'd met during her years in the lab.

''Okay.'' Byron sighed when she failed to respond. ''Give me an example of what it—excuse me—what *he* said to you.''

You're a foolish young girl who takes too many risks.

Paloma gripped the phone and knew she couldn't share anything more. As hard as he'd argued with her before about this move, Byron would go ballistic if she told him everything.

A violent flash of lightning whitened the gray sky, and the telephone crackled just before thunder exploded and shook the earth.

''Paloma!''

She'd ducked instinctively during the flash and gritted her teeth through the thunder. The weather, it seemed, was going to be an unlikely ally and get her out of this difficult situation. ''I'm sorry, Byron. Conditions are deteriorating faster than I'd expected.

I'd better get my supplies and hurry home. We can discuss this when you next visit.''

"Which is going to be in about four hours, if you don't convince me that you're not keeping something from me," Byron declared, in a tone that made it clear he meant business. "Have you been threatened, Paloma?''

There was no way she could answer that question. Just as there was no way she would ever again give up her right to make her own decisions. "I'm fine, Byron. Will you be coming out this weekend?''

"Saturday. You can count on it," he grumbled. "In the meantime, *keep in touch*. If anything unusual happens, I want to hear about it.''

"All right.''

"And then you stay the hell out of those woods.''

She assured him that she would. After thanking him for his input, she hung up, and the smile she'd forced immediately turned into a troubled frown.

Byron's hunch was that she was dealing with a human being, just as her own mind kept wanting her to imagine. But would he continue to think so if he knew about the episode in the woods, or if he had seen those scratches on the compound wall and felt it shake, or had heard that dying animal's cry in the woods? If a person did those things, he would have to be extraordinary, wouldn't he?

More confused than ever, and increasingly uneasy, Paloma raced through an intensifying downpour to her car. She was soaked and shaking by the time she climbed inside. An unexpected gust of wind sent her van rocking sideways. At the same time, it lifted the flimsy roof off the gas station, then slammed it back down on its metal posts, creating a terrible sound more frightening than the thunder.

Oh, Lord, she thought. If the weather was anything like this at the compound, the animals would be in a panic. She had to stop these preoccupations, and hurry back.

Good intentions aside, it was a full half hour later when, her shopping accomplished, she jumped into the van and headed for home. She'd raised eyebrows in her frantic race through the grocery store. Not that she cared. A nagging sense of unease for the welfare of her animals had made people's curiosity over her rather lopsided variety of purchases inconsequential. Let them think what they would. In this day and age of fad diets she thought she almost fit in.

The storm raged on. Never had she seen wind so fierce. It flung the rain in horizontal shoots against the van, creating even more of a challenge to keep it on the road.

Driving should have become easier once she entered the woods, but it didn't. She had to stop several times to drag fallen branches out of the way, which delayed her progress more. Once, at the town lake, something darted across the narrow road, almost causing her to lose control of the car and drive into the water. Had it been a big dog? A calf? It was impossible to tell in the driving rain.

Thankfully, the rain began to slow soon afterward. By the time she finally pulled up before the compound's entrance, the fine drizzle seemed anticlimactic to her pounding heart and surging adrenalin. So was the sun emerging from beneath angry gray clouds in the western sky.

Even so, she hurried to open the gates. That's when she spotted the front door of the house wide open. Dread gripped her anew.

"Harry!" she cried. "Daisy? Ditto!"

What had they done? Where had they gone off to? Her hands were never more clumsy as she struggled to work the key into the lock.

Just as she succeeded in releasing the latch, she heard a cry from the far side of the house. She flung open the gates so hard, they slammed against the wall and bounced back at her.

About to race to see what had happened, one of the chimps came charging around the corner. It was Daisy.

The chimp began screeching and gesturing frantically. Deciding the van could wait, Paloma ran to the frightened creature.

"What wrong?" she asked and signed.

Daisy touched an index finger to the back of her hand twice, her sign for Ditto's name. Then she stretched her arm skyward and let it fall.

"Fall? Ditto fell? Something fell on Ditto!"

Scooping the animal into her arms, she ran. The ground was slippery with mud, and there was no avoiding a few puddles. But Paloma didn't care, except to hope she wouldn't fall and hurt Daisy

She rounded the house, and saw the tree, first. It was the one between the barn and the storage shed. The wind had literally ripped it out of the ground, and it had landed dangerously close to the house. Another few feet and it would have taken out a window or two on the first floor. A small catastrophe for someone like her who knew nothing about repairing windows, let alone the frames.

Whining and squirming in her arms, Daisy pointed. On the far side of the tree's crown, she saw Old Harry attempting to lift one of the tree's branches over his head. Paloma understood immediately what he was trying to do.

Old Harry, wait!

He released the limb and shuffled along the trunk to beckon her closer. *Hair help.*

Where Ditto?

Help Shy Girl.

Paloma experienced another surge of anguish. Except for hers, they rarely used the secret names. She looked around and shook her head. *Where?*

Daisy screeched and pointed to the center of the huge crown and Paloma felt her heart plummet. "Okay, sweetheart, get down. Let Hair see."

Gingerly, she climbed into the sea of leaves and branches, making her way under one branch and over another. As she worked her way deeper into the mass, droplets of cool water showered her already-soaked body.

"Ditto? Ditto, can you hear me?"

The wind was blowing just enough to rustle the leaves on the trees and block out most of her voice. Daisy's cries and Old Harry's guttural input didn't help; however, after a few more cautious maneuverings, she thought she heard a tinny-sounding wail.

"Ditto?"

Yes. She heard it again. Paloma ducked beneath the leaves and peered into the green jungle. A full body-length away, she saw the tipped-over wheelbarrow caught under one of the larger branches.

"Oh, God..." She fought her way closer and stretched as much as she could to scratch the metal belly of the cart. "Ditto? Are you in there?"

A frantic cry came from within the solid prison. Paloma felt herself break out in a sweat. An industrial type of wheelbarrow, even without the tree holding it down, was tough to maneuver. Crushed as it was to the earth by that limb, Paloma also had no idea if Ditto had enough air.

"Okay, Ditto. Stay still," she said, just to let the chimp hear her voice. "Stay quiet. Hair get you out soon."

But how?

She needed a saw. There were some tools in the barn behind the storage shed. She hadn't really checked out what kind or their condition yet, but surely something in there would be useful.

Extricating herself as quickly as she could, she emerged near the orangutan. *Old Harry come. Help find tool.* "Daisy. Stay. Talk to Ditto."

Together she and the orangutan hurried to the barn. Paloma lifted the bar and swung the doors wide for added light. Musty damp air greeted them and Old Harry grunted, unhappy with the environment. Closed dark spaces still upset him, too, and probably always would.

To get his mind off it, Paloma told him what to look for. *Find saw. Saw like knife.*

He went in one direction and she in another. The barn was more of a mess than the house had been. She also had a hunch that most of the good equipment had been stolen by various trespassers. What remained was either broken or rusty. Even the ancient tractor was useless because its tires were flat.

Saw?

Paloma turned. Yes, Old Harry had indeed found one. *Good!*

She took the rusted bow saw and ran back to the tree. Once again she wove her way under and over branches, until she reached the wheelbarrow.

With a reassuring tap against the metal, she called, "I'm back, Ditto. Hold on."

Trying not to let herself focus too much on the answering cry, she set to work on the first branch that had to be removed. Then the next. It wasn't too difficult at first; they were small limbs. Still, the saw was old and worn. Before she got through the last of the thin ones, she was aching and breathing as though she'd been sawing for hours.

It also became apparent that this saw would never cut through the biggest branch.

She shifted around and tried to use her body weight to push it out of the way. Although nearly average in height, she knew she would have to weigh considerably more to even budge it.

Ditto began protesting louder against her confinement. Paloma knew only too well what the chimp had to be feeling because it was forcing her to remember old nightmares as well.

"What do I do?" she whispered, fighting her panic.

She couldn't give up. She'd never quit fighting in her life. One tree wasn't going to defeat her.

Old Harry get rope. She pointed to the barn where they'd seen a good length coiled and hanging on the wall. *Hair get truck. Pull tree.*

It had to work, because it was her only other idea.

She ran as fast as she could to her vehicle, only to find that it had stalled while she'd been working. She tried to restart the engine, but discovered she'd run out of luck. It had to have flooded.

"Damn, damn, damn!" she cried, striking the steering wheel with frustration. This wasn't right. This wasn't *fair*.

The sky was almost clear now, and the angle of the sun brought it directly into her windshield. Blinded, at first she couldn't see what the commotion was about that broke out again in the yard.

She got out and shaded her eyes in time to see Daisy scrambling for the house. She was followed by... *Ditto?*

Both of them were screaming in terror. Paloma called to them, but they ignored her. At least Ditto didn't look injured, she thought, as they disappeared through the front doorway. But how had the chimp gotten free? And where was Old Harry?

She ran to find out.

The sight that greeted her as she came around the corner of the house brought her to an abrupt halt.

Somehow the tree had been moved several feet. The wheelbarrow was turned on its side, and Old Harry peeked out from behind one barn door looking about as upset as the chimps.

Old Harry move tree?

Not.

Who then?

Monster! The orangutan pointed to the wall . . . and the tree whose branches reached far over it. Just as she took a step toward it, the leaves on the lower limbs bent and shook from some great weight.

She broke into a dead run.

CHAPTER FOUR

As she approached the tree, its limbs trembled under the shifting of some tremendous weight. In the next instant, in a blur of shuddering leaves and silver raindrops, she saw a huge dark shape leap. Then she heard the thud of its heavy landing on the other side of the wall. Paloma stumbled against the stone and cement barrier herself a second later, and struck it with her fist.

"Stop!" She had to gasp for breath. "You can't run away again. You *can't!*"

Her lungs were on fire. Her nerves were stretched to the extreme. She couldn't understand this, *his* inexplicable behavior, despite her helpless familiarity with the macabre and the bizarre.

"Won't you even let me thank you?" she whispered, her lips almost touching the rain-cooled stone.

No thanks are necessary.

She felt weak with relief. *You're wrong. Without your help I would never have been able to free Ditto. You saved her life, and I'll always remember that.*

I care nothing for your gratitude.

Then what about friendship?

When he didn't respond, Paloma grimaced knowing she'd been influenced too much by her conversation with Byron. She needed to backtrack and keep things in perspective.

Why did you do it? Why didn't you leave Ditto to suffocate in there, especially after what you said the other day?

From the other side came the sound of gravel crumbling and twigs snapping under a restless, abrupt movement. *You ask too many questions.*

I'm only trying to understand. You strive to make me, us, fear you, and yet you do this wonderful thing. Now you're attempting to frighten us away again.

To make certain that you don't cause more trouble.

Paloma closed her eyes and shook her head. *No. It's more. I feel you sometimes I feel your curiosity... and your sadness.*

The young always overromanticize everything.

Oh, he could be hurtful. *That's the second time you've made a point to remind me of my age or inexperience. Why do you insist on thinking I can't understand you?*

No one can understand me.

Perhaps you're wrong. Perhaps I could help you.

No one can help me.

Paloma gripped a handful of sweatshirt near her heart. *You break my heart with thoughts like that. It makes you seem so alone.*

The strongest man in the world is the man who stands alone.

She gasped. She knew that line! *That's Ibsen.*

All went still on the other side of the wall. She felt his wariness and it reinforced Paloma's conviction: he'd exposed more than he'd intended. Somehow she knew she now had to reassure him.

Please don't let it trouble you that I know you can read.

Why should it trouble me? Anyone can read.

Not the wild beast you try to make me think you are.

Girl... You court my wrath.

What a strange, but beautifully formal way he phrased himself. Dear heaven, she wanted to know him. She wished she could walk through the wall and reach him.

My name's not Girl, it's Paloma.

He began to withdraw. She felt it before she heard the ground protest his weight. She listened to those steps and their cadence. Her heart dilated with excitement.

He walked on two legs!

"My name is Paloma!"

He paused. She could feel him deliberating. Finally, his reply came to her carried on a warm breeze that caressed her feverish brow.

I know. I've always known.

Paloma stayed by the wall until she could no longer feel the slightest trace of him. Then she lingered awhile longer. Amazed. Intrigued. A myriad of emotions rushed through her, tangling in a quixotic dance, confusing, delighting. Most of all intriguing because she'd discovered something profoundly important just now, and she didn't want this moment to end.

It was Old Harry who brought her out of her trance-like state. Having regained some of his usual spunk, he'd abandoned his hiding spot and had joined her at the wall. But the aura that lingered unsettled him. Or perhaps it was a scent too elusive for her vastly inferior olfactory cells. Envying him his highly developed sense, she let him take her hand and pull her toward the house. She had no choice anyway. Orangutans weighed between one-hundred-thirty and two-hundred pounds, and Harry was somewhere on the upper end of that. She was, however, ready to interrogate him.

You saw.

Old Harry concentrated on his handlike feet and shook his head vigorously. *No see Monster.*

Not say Monster. Help Ditto. Call Friend now.

Monster, Friend, same all same. Harry old Jungle Man. Not see good. To elicit greater sympathy, the orangutan pointed to his eyes and rolled back his lips to give her a toothy grin.

How could she help but love this wise and charming creature? He knew exactly which buttons to push to win her over, and that clever message as he'd reminded her of his secret name had done it.

In her readings, she'd long ago learned that the term orangutan came from the Malay words for "man" and "jungle." When Old Harry had first called himself Jungle Man during one of their covert interchanges back at the laboratory, it had begun a series of dialogues wherein she'd eventually learned his first human friend had taught him that word to give him back some of the dignity that captivity had taken away.

"You are a sneak," she declared, following him into the house. "And don't think this discussion is over."

Once again Old Harry played deaf.

The chimpanzees made up for his silence, scurrying over and begging to be lifted and cuddled. Paloma sat down on one of the straight-backed cane chairs by the kitchen table and settled a girl on each thigh.

"Why you go out?" she said, signing as best she could with such an armful. "Hair say stay in. Bad weather very—" She didn't want to frighten them any more than she had to, but *dangerous* was the right word, and so she fisted both hands, then struck the left on the back of the right.

Using the tail of Paloma's braid as a brush, Daisy pretended she was powdering her chin before charmingly pointed out that the rain had stopped. Ditto, on the other hand, simply hugged her bear tighter and hid her face in Paloma's still-damp sweatshirt. From birth Ditto had been the shier, more sensitive of the two sisters, and it didn't surprise Paloma that she'd been the one to get caught under the wheelbarrow. The question was, who had helped? Daisy was always manipulating her sister into doing things that inevitably got her hurt or into trouble, simply because she tried to please so much.

Paloma tried to counter the mischievous sister's coy behavior with sternness. "Daisy put Ditto in wheelbarrow?"

"Me play play."

"Not toy. Ditto get hurt, then Daisy sad."

"Sad sad." Like a coquette, the chimp leaned over and kissed her sister, then tickled her with Paloma's hair to win a kiss back.

"Con artist," Paloma murmured to herself. She motioned for the two to pay attention again. "Who see Friend?"

Ditto whimpered and immediately flung herself against Paloma's chest again to hide.

She took a moment to rock both females, making the throaty purring sound that seemed to appeal to and soothe so many species of animals. "What scare Ditto?" she finally asked. "What see?"

Daisy, always the willing performer, slid off her lap. With arms akimbo and her face distorted into a feral grimace, she stomped in a circle, grunting. Her pantomime would have been humorous, if it hadn't been for whom she was describing.

"Hair no understand."

The chimp repeated the act, then assumed the role of herself by covering her face with her hands and breaking into a high-pitched shriek. Did that mean Ditto's rescuer was frightening to look at, or simply intimidating? Paloma wanted to believe it was the latter, since she, too, had deduced on several occasions that he was rather large.

It took her a moment to simplify her question. "How look?"

Once again Daisy did her threatening march, and once again Ditto hid and whimpered. It wasn't reassuring.

Paloma glanced over to the senior member of their group. The orangutan's benign expression hardly fooled her.

What say Old Harry?

Say belly empty.

She looked from one face to another and wondered if she was being victimized by some primate conspiracy. She didn't want to think so, not after all they'd been through together over the years, not after the risks she'd taken to try to give them a more bearable life. But something about their mystery visitor had made them go incommunicado on her. Whatever it was, it meant Ditto's rescuer was going to remain a mystery awhile longer.

No matter how she tried not to dwell on the matter, it bothered Paloma to be the only one who hadn't seen him. For the rest of the day she remained busy, getting the truck into the compound, then unloading it, and finally putting their supplies away. Through it all, her mind churned continuously.

She tried to identify details about the shadowy figure she'd seen leap down from the tree. She even went outside the wall again to inspect the area and look for prints. Not surprisingly, she found nothing really telling, except to confirm that something of considerable size and weight had landed there.

So he was large. But did his size alone influence the apes' decision to either refuse to describe him, or portray him as some terrifying beast? Although admittedly curious, she cared less about what he looked like, than proving he was a protector of life, not a destroyer.

One thing she had no doubts about. They were equally curious about each other. He could deny it all he liked, but his timely appearance today had convinced her once and for all.

Her big question was, had he been in the area all along? Or had he been some distance away and felt drawn by the same feeling of concern she'd felt while in town? Could he have felt *her* unease?

The thought that they could be that uniquely connected tantalized her imagination. Even the special communication she and Old Harry shared required they be relatively close. What if Ditto's mysterious savior could read her thoughts from anywhere? Did that mean she might learn to read his?

The idea filled her with wonder. But most of all, Paloma was puzzled by his last message to her. What had he meant when he'd confided that he already knew her name, and had always known it?

That night, mentally and physically exhausted, Paloma looked forward to bed. The others were already fast asleep, their own eventful day taking its toll.

She, too, had no trouble succumbing to the reassuring embrace of sleep. Nestling comfortably under a light blanket, she was about to drift off when she thought she'd heard a whisper.

Paloma.

Instantly alert, she listened. How odd, she thought; gazing up at the textured ceiling. That couldn't have come from Old Harry or one of the girls. They simply didn't use that name for her. Perhaps she'd been more asleep than she'd believed. Perhaps she'd already begun to dream and had been replaying the day's adventures in her head.

Then she heard it again and knew she'd guessed wrong.

"Oh, my," she whispered, enchanted.

He was thinking about her, saying her name in his mind. Saying it, as though it was a flavor to be tasted, rolled over the tongue. Rolled slowly. Tasted wistfully.

She felt it as much as heard it, and the experience spawned such a sensation of intimacy that her body awoke and left her tingling all over. Eager to reassure him, she responded in kind.

I hear you. I'm here.

She shouldn't have done it. He reacted like someone who'd suddenly discovered he'd exposed too much, had revealed a vulnerability too deep, or too raw. Quickly, fiercely, he shut off his mind, locking her out.

Paloma pressed her hands flat against the mattress, glad she was lying down. For a moment she felt ... more than jarred, she felt in limbo. Dizzy. As though he'd sucked the air out of the room in his hasty retreat, leaving her wingless, to find her balance and make sense of things as best she could.

Why had he reacted that way? Why the rejection? Hadn't he realized she would hear him?

An intriguing thought entered her mind. What if he hadn't known? Could it mean that he was no more an expert of this pioneering science than she?

It had to be the most profound experience she'd had since ... well, since she'd been a child and had realized she had telepathic abilities. Clairaudience, she later learned it was called. Those who seriously studied such a phenomenon defined it as the ability to hear another's thoughts. But more than that, at certain times, to experience another's feelings as well.

Recovering somewhat, Paloma sighed and rolled over onto her stomach. If only the connection had lasted long enough for her to discover where he'd been at that moment. She had a feeling he hadn't been close.

It seemed to take forever, on the other hand he had nothing but time. Only when he felt she'd fully succumbed to sleep did he dare access her mind again. Wary, because this was a new phenomenon and he'd yet to grow comfortable with it. Determined, because his fascination would not let him rest until he had more information.

The experience reminded him of one he'd had when he'd been very young, after reading the picture book about the mirror that spoke. Suddenly it had struck him that there were no mirrors in the cave. Right then and there he'd realized he'd always been dissuaded from seeking out his reflection . . . and knew he must see it. Just once.

And that had been the day he'd run off into the woods, to the tiny pool leading off from the stream, where he'd finally viewed what he was.

Fate's newest lesson was no lesser a torment. Admittedly, he'd believed the ability to communicate without actually speaking to her had been unusual, but only until he recalled how easily he understood the mind-set of the other woods dwellers. This, however, was far more distinctive, and troublesome.

Space, time, had no meaning for the two of them.

Why not?

Why him?

Why *her?*

With increasing regularity he could hear her thoughts before she spoke them. Just as she'd heard his after that tree disaster. At *will,* damn it. What a curse. What a farce! Never had two more incompatible souls been linked. The reviled and the innocent. If it wasn't so terrifying, he would laugh.

He didn't want to be lured into this web of temptation. He wanted to throw back his head and roar into the night skies. Loud enough to shake the heavens and crumble the rocks beneath his feet.

But first, just once more, he needed to experience this rare sensation, this special *oneness* that frightened as much as it threatened to make his heartstrings crack.

He leaned back against the rocks, closed his eyes, and cleared his conscious mind of everything. Even the night and the stars. Even his isolation. He let his spirit open and expand like a spring flower to the first rays of morning sun. The rest happened as easily as if she'd suddenly materialized before him....

She slept, but restlessness ensnared her in a hot, humid shroud. He understood the feeling well, for it wasn't unlike his own. Slightly feverish, she twisted against the confinement of the bed covers until she'd kicked her legs free.

Better. She calmed somewhat, liking the cool night's caress. She could be, he was discovering as he sensed her subconscious mind begin spinning images, a highly sensual, if innocent being.

The yearning for more sensory pleasure coaxed her to imagine she was strolling in the woods at dusk. Not exactly these woods, he noted wryly, they were lusher, the vegetation more tropical. Like the plants he'd once seen in the strange picture box, while peeking in a window in the village. The picture box he'd later discovered was called a TV. Man-made magic useless to him.

She walked barefoot and wore the thin shirt she wore now. Hardly longer than her hair, it bared legs that were slender, and smooth. She moved like a deer, her fluid, economic gait enhancing her sleekness and grace.

She filled him with wonder, and made him ache. Both in unfamiliar ways. Different than seeing a rainbow. Different than when he went too long without food.

Better.

Worse.

What could she be searching for? He could tell she didn't know, simply hurried along the soft footpath, peering into the dense brush, all the while a faint, hopeful smile playing around her mouth and lighting her eyes.

How mesmerized he'd been the first time he'd seen her face. She'd looked like the moon itself, luminous and perfect. Pure. She'd tempted him in a frightening way.

He'd been hungry that day, so hungry, and she'd been so... accessible. Momentarily tempted, his savage nature had teetered on the brink of taking control. But something had stopped him. Conscience? Self revulsion? Whatever the case, he'd let her pass.

And now he had to accept that nothing had changed, except to grow more complicated. Today he'd again behaved like some great guard dog. If he didn't take care, he thought with no small scorn, she could soon put a collar and chain on him, the way the villagers did their tamed beasts.

She shifted and uttered a soft protest, picking up on his agitation. It was yet another reminder that the connection worked both ways.

With quiet returning, she settled again. The dream regained control. This time when the images came, he could actually sense whom she was seeking.

He sat forward, his excitement—although there was tension, too—intensifying. *Me. She's looking for me.*

How sweet her thoughts were. How inviting. And what rapture he would feel to pretend, if only for an instant, that dreams like this could come true. Because he'd never been desired. He never would be. But he craved it, craved it with all his soul.

She came to some thicker brush. He almost nodded in recognition. The berry patch. Seeing the place through her eyes had him staring at glossy, fan-shaped leaves, enhanced by huge pink and white flowers that gave off an intoxicating fragrance. A young girl's version of romance. What in heaven's name did she expect to see when she parted those branches?

His heart began to pound. As she reached out, he found himself holding his breath.

A hand inched toward her, offering her one of the exotic blossoms. The look on her face... He still couldn't make himself breathe, but now it was for a different reason. Such joy, such welcome. But something was wrong.

The hand.

It was just as he'd expected. Dreaded. Despite all that she'd been through, regardless of hearing what she had while trespassing in his territory, ignoring what she subconsciously understood to be the truth, she'd chosen to see him as... normal. So normal.

She beckoned him to step from his hiding place. Instead, he presented her with one of her animals, the small creature he'd freed today from its suffocating trap. The chimpanzee begged a flower from her, and then ran off into the woods with it.

A pretty scene. An innocent's fantasy.

He didn't want to see anymore. His imagination was brutal enough without watching hers decimate him further. But he couldn't stop, either. Somehow his fascination with *her* was far stronger than his need to protect himself.

Accepting her hand, a figure stepped from the lush vegetation. He was tall, dark, magnificent in form and visage. A perfect foil to her untouched beauty, and as far from reality as anything she could have conceived.

With an anguished moan, he distanced his mind. Pushing himself away from the rocks, he vowed, no more. She would destroy him with her innocent fantasies.

But even as he started for the cave, he stopped himself.

How could he go in yet? His feral mood would attract attention. Raise questions. Would he lie to protect himself? To protect her?

Sweet heaven, why? He had so little to call his own, why must it all be wrapped pain? And how long was *she* going to deceive herself?

He sat back down. Drawing a deep breath, he once again accepted the connection. Immediately, he winced. She was gazing up at her fantasy hero, at *him*, with adoration and trust, and he knew she wanted to be touched. Kissed.

When she lifted her small, graceful hands and rested them against his chest, dear God, he felt them. A rush of delicious torment swept through him.

Slowly, she let her eyes drift closed, until raven-black lashes swept low over her flushed cheeks. Then she parted her lips.

A need as old as time and as painful as any he'd ever known gripped him and threatened to squeeze the air from his lungs.

He'd never known ecstasy. Now he'd glimpsed what it could be like. And there could be more. She could show him it all through her imagination, if he let her.

But it wouldn't be *him* she would be responding to. Could he spend the rest of his days knowing he'd shared in what wasn't rightfully his to experience?

No, reality was much better. Bitterly, he allowed his own subconscious greater control. She had to learn never to do this to him, to *them,* again.

He concentrated—and suddenly, the hands that held her were not so clean, or handsome. Not so safe. The mouth that had begun to lower toward hers twisted into a feral, lusting snarl, and redirected its aim to her delicate throat.

Startled, she opened her eyes, and he watched knowledge flicker to life in those alluring dark pools. Sheer terror, dread, and disgust followed.

It still wasn't enough.

He would prove to her once and for all that she was not welcome in his woods, in his world, in his head! With a fierce roar, he ripped the soft cloth covering her, rending it in two. The force of his jerk brought her to her knees, and he leered at her glorious young body. His own throbbed with a hunger too long denied.

You wanted this. Take it. Take me!

No—no! She fought, she screamed, she begged. *Oh, please. You don't mean this. You helped me. You protected us. I know you did.*

She tried to stop him. Her efforts, of course, were wasted. No one could match his strength or cunning. Little could stop him, except, perhaps, a bullet, and there had yet to be someone bold and brave enough to do him that favor.

But he would do her one by teaching her never to dare dream of him again.

"No!"

Paloma sat bolt upright in bed, her screams still echoing in her ears. It took her a moment to realize part of that was due to the chimps, who'd also awakened with cries. And so had Old Harry. The grip of panic was total, and lingered.

Despite the sweat that had her nightshirt clinging to her body, and a barely suppressible impulse to pull the sheet over her head and curl into a tight ball, the moment her companions ran to her, Paloma spread her arms to embrace them. Because, she reminded herself, they were all she had, just as she was all they had. But she could only manage hugs, since right now words of reassurance were beyond her.

What had that creature been? Why had it invaded her dream? Up until its interference, everything had seemed so pleasant, so sweet, so... perfect.

What Hair see?

Paloma knew she had to pull herself together. She stroked Old Harry's back, pretended to find and pluck off a burr in his hair. As the books Byron had lent her attested, grooming worked faster than anything in calming a stressed primate.

Nothing. Bad dream. Gone now.

Old Harry think Monster come.

No come. Bad dream.

A bad dream she had no explanation for, nor did she want to think that anything as terrible as she'd envisioned could actually exist, or that it could act so viciously. As far as her experiences had taught her, only humans were that heartless, that brutal.

Most important, why had her subconscious twisted her beautiful dream into something ugly and frightening? She occasionally still had nightmares about Isaac, but at least she understood why they occurred. With Byron's help, she'd even learned how to control them. Most of them at any rate.

Today had been stressful, true, and that could have spawned a bad dream. But things had ended—if not happily, then at least not *un*happily.

All right, she allowed with chagrin, she had been surprised at how she'd turned Ditto's rescuer into such a romantic figure, especially since she'd never allowed herself the childish luxury of playing "pretend" before. It could be that her subconscious had overcompensated while trying to correct the matter. But there was no emotional reason for the dream to turn so bizarre or get so out of hand.

Unless there was something deeper going on here that she wasn't tuning into.

Confused as she might be, the chimps recovered and soon grew sleepy again. Paloma carried them one by one to their cot. Afterward, she roused Old Harry just enough to help him shuffle off to his chair.

Wide awake herself, she soothed her restless spirit by wandering around the house. Although she'd already checked them, she yielded to the impulse to make sure the windows and doors were secured.

Not surprisingly, they were.

She paused by the kitchen window, touched the blossom on one geranium and almost reluctantly lifted her gaze out into the darkness. Tonight she felt very much alone, and wished she wasn't.

Are you out there?

Somewhere an owl hooted. It wasn't the response she'd hoped for.

Feeling a bit chilled, she added a log to the wood-burning stove, then slipped back into bed. Covering herself, she curled into a fetal position not unlike Ditto's. A deep melancholia was replacing her earlier fear, and she knew it would be a long time before sleep would return.

She gazed across the dark room, but her eyes searched for someone far beyond the chipped plaster walls. She could almost feel him. Almost.

If you're trying to frighten me, you succeeded. For a moment. But it wasn't because of how you looked, it was because of how you responded. To me, you'll never be ugly.

CHAPTER FIVE

There was a price to be paid for the day's and night's experiences. Paloma discovered it when the next day passed and the next, and they had no more contact with their mysterious visitor. Although she tried not to let her thoughts dwell on him, just as she tried to put her bad dream behind her, she wondered if, perhaps frustrated with her decision to stay in the area, he'd chosen to leave himself. Admittedly confounded by the whole situation, she was ready and eager for Byron's visit on Saturday to help get her mind off things.

He drove up to the gates in the mid-morning, creating a mild uproar among her animals. They'd grown deeply fond of Byron over the past year. Back at the farm, he'd made a point to help care for them whenever possible, not only because he'd insisted Paloma needed the relief, but because he genuinely loved animals.

"What did you do, leave Portland before dawn?" Paloma called, as she unlocked and opened the gates. She was glad to see him, despite the tension that had underscored most of their conversation the other day.

"Almost," he shot back, leaning out the window of his four-wheel-drive vehicle. The sun lit his wavy brown hair to a burnished gold. With the twin dimples on either side of his mouth deepening, he looked more like a graduate student than a doctor. "Flattered?"

"Absolutely." With an affectionate smile, she stepped out of the way to watch him drive in.

He parked near the pump by the front walk, and as soon as he climbed out, he spent several minutes playing with Old Harry and the girls. Dressed in his usual uniform of crisp blue jeans and a polo shirt in immaculate white, which made her feel gauche in her worn-but-comfortable green sweat suit, the sensitive and athletic man finally relented to the apes' childlike entreaties to present the treats they'd come to expect from him.

"It's about time you gave in," Paloma said, from her perch on the edge of the water trough. As he approached her, she straightened and extended her arms. "I noticed a distinct gleam in Old Harry's eyes and worried he was going to take matters into his own hands. I imagine replacing a door on something like this thing would cost even a coveted young research scientist like you a pretty penny."

Byron grimaced. "You've got a point."

With a silent laugh, Paloma hugged him. "It's good to see you, friend."

He embraced her and murmured into her ear, "Same here, kiddo. How've you been?"

"Can't complain."

He leaned back and tapped the tip of her nose. "This is going to grow if you try to hand me a whitewash like that."

"I *am* fine," Paloma insisted, believing it was true—if she ignored a few disconcerting things in her life. "And I'm even finer now that you're here."

"Flattery will get you a lot, but I have to tell you that you look beat."

"I never sleep well during a full moon, you know that." She hooked her arm through his and started toward the back of the truck. "Come along. You know you're going to lose points with this bunch, if you don't give them what they want."

Although she could sense his speculative, worried gaze still on her, Byron let her lead him. Lifting the back door, he handed the delighted chimps pink ponies on wheels, and presented Old Harry with his "pretty"—a child's fringed parasol.

"Oh, my," Paloma murmured, fighting back a laugh as Byron helped the orangutan open it and showed him how to hold it. Old Harry grinned and wandered off in a definite swagger. "There'll be no living with him now. You spoil them all."

"Well, I try, but I'm not so sure how successful I am."

Something in the tone of his voice had her glancing back at him, and she saw the leather-bound set of Jane Austen novels in his hands.

"Byron." She shook her head. "How did you guess?"

The dimples that gave his smooth face such charm deepened. "Oh, it wasn't all that difficult. I know you're a romantic at heart, and I also know you wouldn't have much of an opportunity to find anything like this in Vickery. And don't forget, that was *my* paperback copy of *Pride and Prejudice* that you wore out back at the farm."

Dear Byron. If only she could give him a sign of hope, he would move heaven and earth to make her happy. What he failed to accept is that even if she could love him that way, she would also be haunted by guilt for burdening him with the threat of retaliation by Isaac. Her guardian turned nemesis was still out there, somewhere, possibly looking for her. Paloma doubted that Isaac would ever give up until he found her—or death found him first.

"I'm glad you remember my sins," she murmured, kissing his cheek lightly. "Come inside while I put these out of their reach," she added, tilting her head toward her primate friends who were too involved with their own presents to pay attention. "Are you hungry? Thirsty?"

Byron assured her that he was neither, having driven through a fast-food stop along the way. But he carried inside a treat for *her*, an ice chest of perishables packed down by crushed cubes. In turn, he picked up the empty one from his last visit.

"Now you'll have some milk, cheese and eggs for a few days," he told her.

He'd been worrying about her nutritional habits ever since she'd confided that her diet at her uncle's had been unorthodox at best, and that even free, she focused more on the animals' meals than her own. Paloma set the books on the shelf over her cot, thinking about how Old Harry would beg for the eggs, and try to steal the cheese if the opportunity presented itself. That was something she decided she had better keep to herself.

"I do appreciate it, Byron, but you shouldn't spend all your hard-earned money on us, or bring so much," she scolded gently, as she returned to the kitchen area.

"Who else do I have to spend it on?" he asked with a dismissive shrug.

Paloma smiled again, but secretly felt guilty. She'd hoped this move would force him to see how he'd been neglecting his personal life, but apparently the old adage about absence making the heart grow fonder was still holding true.

Concerned that their conversation might get too personal, Paloma coaxed him back outside under the pretense of having to keep an eye on the animals. Daisy, having mastered riding her toy horse, rolled past a regal Old Harry, who sat on the grass, his umbrella angled jauntily over his head. As he spotted them, the orangutan stared meaningfully at Byron.

"What's he telling me?" Byron asked.

She knew he possessed no telepathic skills, but he'd been around Harry long enough to recognize the sidelong glances that usually meant the process was going on. She, of course, had picked up the communication immediately, and the orangutan's message had her insides doing aerial acrobatics.

Monster carry great tree.

It gave her no pleasure to have to deceive Byron, but her response to Old Harry was blunt. *No tell.*

Friend speak Friend.

No.

Openly disgruntled, Old Harry turned his back to her and lowered the parasol to hide himself from their view. Paloma knew she would have some pacifying to do later, but thought it the easier of her options. She simply refused to upset Byron.

"Did you pick it up?" he asked.

She summoned a dry smile for him. "Oh, he's just tattling on the girls' transgressions. Let's go over to the side of the house." Paloma took his arm and led him in the opposite direction of the orangutan. "I want your suggestion about something."

He went willingly enough, but came to an abrupt halt the moment he saw the felled tree. In the last few days, Paloma had tried to saw off what branches she could, and to clean up the mess as best as she could, but she hadn't had much success.

"What on earth happened?" Byron demanded, scowling as he looked from the tree, to the house, then to her. "Why didn't you tell me about this?"

"How could I? It happened while I was in town. Remember the day I phoned you?"

"Right, the storm," he murmured and whistled softly. "You're lucky it came down at a slight angle. If it had fallen straight, you would have had an enormous amount of damage on the house to deal with. Were the animals all right when you got back?"

Paloma didn't have to glance around to know Old Harry had decided to follow them. "They were shaken, but basically all right."

Old Harry good tell story.

She forced herself to ignore him, and said to Byron, "I was wondering if you could suggest a way to get rid of this, short of investing in a chain saw. I've done all I can with the old bow saw I found in the barn."

"And that's more than you should have done. I wish you would have gone back into town and called me, I could have picked up or borrowed a decent saw."

"You do enough as it is. Besides, after seeing what could have happened, I wasn't about to leave them again. I just wanted you to tell me if I needed an ax or—"

"Ax? Be serious. You don't think you can tackle something this huge on your own? And with an ax no less . . ."

His sarcasm, unintentional as it may have been, hurt and annoyed her. She folded her arms beneath her breasts. How could he have forgotten that it was "little old her" who'd planned and plotted for days, months, years to free herself and the chimps and Harry from the laboratory? Every day she did the work of two people, faced crises he couldn't begin to imagine. Did he think she was going to be undone by a giant lump of wood?

"I know I can handle it."

He would have to have been deaf to miss the quiet resolve in her voice. She could also see he was remembering some of the stories she'd told him about their existence at Isaac's, how sometimes they'd lost track of days at a time because her guardian used the effective punishment of darkness and isolation, then withheld food until she scrubbed down the cages and floors with nothing more than a pail, a brush and a mop.

Byron grimaced and then took hold of her upper arms. "This isn't about survival," he said gently, apologetically. "I know you can handle a great deal, and have. This is about muscle, pure and simple."

Paloma knew she'd overreacted, but past experiences had taught her to be terrified of not only losing her and the apes' freedom, but her self-control. "I'm sorry. I know you're one of the good guys."

"I shouldn't have sounded so bossy," Byron replied, stroking her shoulders with his thumbs. Abruptly, he dropped his hands and cleared his throat. "Ah, let me think.... I have a rope in the trunk for emergencies. Why don't I tie it to the bumper and drag the tree into the woods?"

Paloma hated the thought of the waste. "I'd like to use it for firewood."

"It's too green."

"True, but if I stacked it near the front door somewhere, it could season for later. It would definitely save me time and energy in the winter."

From his expression, Paloma could tell Byron didn't want to think about her spending the winter here. But just as quickly, he gave her a curt nod.

"Okay. I'll move it along the wall over there." He pointed to the area near the supply shed. "Then we'll worry about cutting it up next time I come out."

Paloma eyed the location. It was where their elusive visitor had entered the compound on more than one occasion. Would having the tree there help or hinder his access?

"All right," she murmured, silently chastising herself for her rambling thoughts. "Thanks."

Never would she have guessed moving one tree could turn into such a production. Since a single individual had managed to shift the entire tree, Paloma reasoned that a truck would have no difficulty dragging the remaining portion. She was wrong.

The longer she stood and watched the truck's tires spinning and kicking up dirt and gravel, the greater her respect and awe for what Ditto's rescuer had accomplished. How on earth had he managed it?

Inevitably, the chimps joined her and Old Harry. Several times Paloma could feel the orangutan's gaze. She tried to ignore him, but finally relented.

What?

Monster strong.

Yes, very, she thought, feeling her palms grow damp as she thought of the size of the shadowy figure she'd glimpsed on two occasions. Could there be such a being that had the shoulder span of two average men and stood at least a full head or more taller? No, her eyes had to have been playing tricks on her.

Byron finally succeeded in getting the tree parallel to the wall. Pleased with himself, he joined the group and surveyed his handiwork while brushing off his hands. "That's much better, don't you think?"

Paloma thanked him again, trying not to notice that Daisy had begun the pantomime she'd performed the other day. That sent Ditto running to Paloma to hide behind her leg. Naturally, Byron noticed.

"Hey, will you look at that. I guess I should be flattered."

Old Harry shot her a speaking glance, making it all the more difficult to respond. She managed a smile and nod, then focused on lifting and quieting the whimpering Ditto in her arms.

"Daisy stop," she scolded, the other chimp. "Go get toy. Play nice."

Daisy, however, liked all the attention she was getting and continued her act, which made Ditto all the more upset. Byron became more interested, especially when Old Harry turned his back on the whole scene and pretended a great preoccupation with his parasol.

"Do you think Ditto's trying to tell you something else, something more?" he asked after a few moments of somber observation.

"No, I think she just enjoys teasing her sister." But as soon as she spoke, Daisy pointed to the wall, jumped up and down, and shrieked noisily. Paloma wanted to groan.

If she hadn't said anything the other day to Byron about her expanding abilities, he might never have given Daisy's performance a second thought. Now, however, he followed Daisy's directions and glanced toward the wall, then back at the chimpanzee. "Has there been more trouble?" he asked quietly.

She could feel herself being pulled in different directions. The very idea of having to lie again to Byron made her physically ill, and if he found out she'd been less than truthful, the damage it could cause their relationship might be irrevocable. But if she told him about what had happened, he would undoubtedly subject her to enormous pressure to leave here and go to Portland with him. Beyond the worry about how much attention an orangutan and two chimps would garner in a populated area, that arrangement would also resurrect the problem of keeping their relationship carefully defined.

There was also another problem, whether Isaac Tredway ever found them again or not. The fact was, she knew she couldn't live the way other people did. She'd spent too many years apart from the mainstream of society, and too many creating her own.

"Trouble?" she murmured evasively, still trying to make a decision. "Oh, you mean about picking up that other voice? Um...no. I believe it's gone." At least that much was true. For the last few days she'd felt nothing whatsoever.

"Are you sure? Maybe you missed it," Byron added, glancing from the chimps to her. "Do you suppose they could have witnessed something while you were in town? Besides the tree, I mean."

"Well . . ."

Beware.

Startled, Paloma shifted her free hand to her throat. It was *him!* He'd come back.

"Paloma?"

Byron's disturbed glance forced her to take a firmer grip on her quixotic emotions. "I'm sorry, I was remembering how upset they were when I got home and found the tree down." The conflict between feeling both elated and traitorous was not a pleasant experience at all. "I really do think that episode's behind us, Byron."

Old Harry saved her from having to explain more by pointing to the house. *Go inside. Inside safe go.*

"Ah—Harry wants something cool to drink. Why don't we all have something?" she suggested brightly. "It's time to show you this month's journals, anyway."

It was that easy, and that disconcerting. Byron went along willingly, as did the chimps and Old Harry, except that they were far more subdued. They also refused to go outside after their refreshments, for good reason, of course, but it made it more difficult to review her work with Byron.

About two hours later, after some intense reading under less than ideal conditions, he snatched up a tablet and pen and began scribbling notes for her.

"You're still not getting it," he grumbled. "I want you to reach for something more."

"More?" she asked, straightening after taking one of her journals away from Daisy. Getting a bit frustrated herself, she blew a strand of hair out of her face.

"Complex."

"You're not pleased with our progress?"

He gestured toward the book in front of him. "From all indications, they're still locked in on imitative sentence formats. Things like "See go see" and "Pretty me have pretty" have been achieved to the point where the scientific community refuses to be impressed by it. I need you to concentrate on encouraging them to invent their own subject-predicate sequences. I'm looking for greater lingual dexterity. The more creative the better."

"Are you sure you don't want them to write you the great American novel while they're at it?" Paloma asked, frowning at his blunt, dismissive tone.

She couldn't help it, she was proud of her animals' achievements and felt each new word of learned communication—regardless of its sequence or repetitive pattern—was a miracle to be marveled at, not shrugged away. It didn't make her question Byron's friendship or his commitment to her animals' continued safety, but she felt she was glimpsing someone who'd lost sight of the magic these special beings possessed. She might as well be listening to a computer!

Byron grimaced and ran his hand through his hair. "I know, you think I sound like an insensitive jerk who's not mindful of all you've accomplished. Nothing could be further from the truth. The rapport you've achieved among the four of you is phenomenal.

"But at the same time," he added, leaning forward in his chair, as he grew even more earnest, "you must understand the dilemma I'm facing. I'm painfully aware that it's nothing for a primate to learn dozens, hundreds of words. They can ask for food easily enough. What *I'm* looking for is the animal that will reject a banana and ask for a cookie because he likes the taste of the sweet better. That's when we'll *really* know we've locked onto something that might prove reasoning ability."

Might? Paloma already knew her animals were capable of reasoning. Harry had been doing so when he'd spoken to her for the first time nine years ago. And even the other day when he'd indicated he wanted nuts instead of fruit, his cunning mind had been sharper than some humans she'd met. Perhaps much of his message had been communicated in a repetitive nature, but so what? She heard people all the time who constantly began sentences with "Well," or ended them with "you know." Did that mean *they* weren't reasoning?

Did she want to share that with Byron yet?

He knew much about her and the animals' past, and had always been supportive and sympathetic. Paloma believed he only wanted the best for them. But what if one of his superiors wanted Old Harry or one of the chimps to be brought in for an examination or observation someday? Would Byron be able to protect them then? She'd promised that never again would her vulnerable friends be subjected to cages or a laboratory environment. Would she be able to keep her word if she shared more of their intelligence with the world?

She wished she'd have thought of all this before, but too naive, foolish or simply *young,* she hadn't. The fact was, she'd been too busy trying to keep a roof over their heads and food in their bellies.

She needed to be more cautious, to reexamine their situation, including obtaining some new reassurances from Byron. She still trusted him more than anyone in the world, but she had great doubts about the profession he served.

How complicated life was becoming. It wasn't fair, especially when there was much more to deal with, namely the mystery outside their compound.

"I see your point," Paloma finally said to Byron, deciding a neutral answer would buy her the time she needed. "And I'll see what I can do."

Byron stayed until late afternoon. As soon as he closed her journals, he became the smiling, considerate friend she'd first trusted. Although the rest of their visit was enjoyable, the more the sun descended, the more anxious Paloma became for him to leave. The feeling became a fear, when she caught a movement out of the corner of her eye and thought she saw a shadowy figure by one of the windows.

When Byron finally admitted he had to start back, Paloma nearly sighed with relief. As they emerged from the house, she virtually held her breath, but she should have known better. The yard was empty.

"Do you promise to leave that tree until I can get out here with a chain saw next week?" Byron asked with mock sternness as he opened his truck door.

"Absolutely." Paloma rocked Ditto, who was exhausted from trying to please them so much during her lessons. "Unless I'm in need of a toothpick—then no guarantees."

"Cute." He backtracked and kissed her very close to her lips. "Take care of yourself," he added, his voice husky.

Her eyes burned from repressed tears as she watched him leave. Closing the gates after him, she had to acknowledge it was because they'd lost something between them during this visit. And it was her fault.

Why do you cry?

The awkward, barely audible query had her glancing around for Old Harry. They'd left him inside, napping on his chair. Daisy lay on a patch of still-warm grass, content to roll her pony back and forth before her. Her heavy-lidded eyes indicated she would be asleep herself in a minute or two. That meant only one thing.

Blinking away the welling tears she took another step along the compound wall, shifting the limp Ditto to hold her more protectively against her. She hoped the abruptly fiercer pounding of her heart didn't rouse the chimp.

Heavens, was she losing all her self-preservation instincts? Why hadn't she told Byron that *he'd* been close for hours now? Why wasn't she terrified? Granted, she felt something akin to fear, vibrations that raced through her like staccato notes on a piano. But muting it was something stronger, and it pulled her toward the area near the downed tree.

She stopped. Listened. "You haven't left. Will you speak to me?"

A deep, expansive silence spread over the compound and the surrounding woods. No animals sang afternoon songs. None flew over their block of sky. She knew what that meant and it helped her wait for him to make up his mind.

"Please," she entreated. "I didn't betray your presence earlier, did I?"

"You almost told."

His voice didn't float over the high wall, it permeated it like thunder, and reverberated in her chest. Paloma stood mesmerized.

"No," she replied, "I didn't. I debated, then chose to protect you."

"Because you knew I was close and could retaliate."

"You think so?" She touched her cheek to Ditto's soft, fuzzy hair. "You aren't getting better at understanding me, at all."

"And you're assuming a great deal. What makes you think I didn't wait for your friend to leave so that I could attack at leisure? No one to hear your cries. No one to help."

The threat was eerie because he spoke with a casualness reminiscent of her uncle's cool delivery. Ditto stirred slightly, picking up on her unease. "Please stop. I told you before you've succeeded in frightening me."

"Not enough. You still won't leave."

"Because I know what's outside those front gates frightens me more than you do."

A throaty growl underscored a faint breeze. "You tempt me to show you how wrong you are. Make no mistake, I'm not one of your pets!"

The idea was so far from what she felt, she couldn't help but shake her head. "I've never thought that, nor do I see these poor creatures as *pets*. We have too much in common for me to insult them with that label. We're all refugees. All orphans. We belong nowhere and to no one."

Realizing she'd begun to raise her voice, she took a deep breath and crooned to Daisy, who'd made a mewing protest. It was wrong for her to get so agitated at him. The only way any life-form could live in harmony with another was if everyone acknowledged everyone else's right to their own space.

"You think like a child, a dreamer."

Not at all surprised that he'd stealthily crept into her thoughts again, pride demanded Paloma defend herself. "I think as an idealist, which is nothing to be ashamed of."

"See how far it serves you as armor."

She knew his muttered response held considerable truth, but she was too world-weary to argue philosophy with him. Besides, their exchanges were stressful enough as it was.

"Why were you crying?"

She'd already sensed that he hadn't wanted to ask, so why had he repeated the question? Paloma felt as though this whole situation with him was drawing her into a surreal world.

"It's complicated," she said at last.

"You smile at him, but your visitor makes you unhappy."

Rattled, she stared at the wall. *He saw?*

"Byron means well, and we—*I* owe him a great deal. He all but saved our lives at a time when we didn't know where to turn."

"But he disappoints you."

Paloma bit her lip and looked to the sky for stability. "He belongs to another world."

A soft gasp pierced the air, followed by a deeper silence than before. Aware of it, drawn by something inexplicable, Paloma leaned against the sun-warmed wall as though it were a sturdy shoulder. "What? What's wrong?"

"Nothing," he muttered. "It mustn't be allowed to matter."

"What mustn't matter?"

"That words flow so easily from your lips, only to rip at my soul. That what troubles your heart like an unquiet eddy, affects mine."

"What do you believe should matter?" she whispered, feeling caught in some time warp while sunset painted the sky shades of fiery orange.

"Reality. I must go."

"No—not yet!"

"You torment me."

"I'm trying to *understand*."

"Understand this," he snarled. "I stalk when I'm hungry, and kill when I'm threatened. The rest..."

Paloma waited, aware her clothes were clinging to her back. She shut her eyes. "The rest?"

CHAPTER SIX

Why had he answered?

He should never have answered.

He stalked the woods for hours, waiting for the physical and emotional shield of darkness. Then he wandered farther trying to forget.

It was late when he returned to the cave. The oil lanterns were already lit, and they filled the cavern with a soft welcoming light that guided his step, and should have warmed his heart, but didn't.

Without a word, he carried his bounty down the slope to the table he'd confiscated—along with other things—from the previously abandoned estate. As he carefully set down his armload of goods, his shadow was joined by a much smaller one.

"You've been to the village."

He didn't look at her. The lack of inflection in her voice told him more than he wanted to know. Besides, they rarely looked at each other. There was no need after all these years.

"I'd wondered what was keeping you," she added, when he failed to respond.

"We needed the food."

"You took risks in order to avoid hunting."

They had few secrets between them, a condition forced upon them as a result of their habitat, as much as their respect for each other. But he did resent the suggestion that he'd shirked his responsibility to her.

"We needed the fresh produce."

"What I need is fresh meat. Skins. You seem to forget that winter is never far away."

"I'll get it for you, only not *tonight*."

His barely controlled temper obviously had little effect on her. She cast him a somber, sidelong look. "What happened today?"

He exhaled in frustration. Recognizing the need for space, he spun away from her and sprawled across a long length of ledge to the left of her. "Why is it that whenever anything doesn't please you, you think something has to have happened?"

"Because I know you. I know your strengths and I know your weaknesses, few though they are." She began sorting through the mass of fruits and vegetables. "And I know about how restless and sensitive you've become since *she* moved into that house down below. Now tell me—what happened today?"

He still couldn't bring himself to discuss Paloma with her. It would be easier to tear off his own skin.

"I think we'd better discuss her because she's making you moody and reckless."

"No one saw me in the village," he replied, a warning in his voice. "I was careful."

"Perhaps." She stared at a cantaloupe as though studying a crystal ball. "But the point is that until she came, you've never gone near Vickery at this hour. You've always been mindful that people could be moving about. And you've never gone without warning me first."

He sat up. Scowled. "Is that what this is all about? You're annoyed because I didn't report my decision to you?"

"It's been a long time since I've had to remind you that you're not like others."

It had riled him that she'd remained unperturbed to the warning in his voice. Now she bruised him further by bringing up what didn't need to be recalled. "Not since I was a boy, afraid to go out into the light because I felt ugly, and ashamed," he said bitterly.

"Because you were responsible. More responsible and considerate about your welfare and mine than you are now."

"Will you let me be!" He lunged off the ledge and at the table, striking it with his fist. "I'll get you your meat. I'll make certain you have new skins before winter. I'll do whatever necessary. Just leave me alone!"

Fruit and vegetables leapt into the air, and shot off the table like marbles. And then came the popping sound as the pine table split down the center.

Disgusted with his loss of control, he flung himself away from the scene. He hated that he had failed her. Snatching up one of the lanterns, he raced through the craggy aperture that led to the unfathomed depths of the earth.

"Wait!"

He ignored the cry. He knew it worried her when he ventured down here. But it couldn't matter right now.

Another narrow path sliced naturally into the wall face of this inner cavern, twisting and turning like some mad architect's spiral staircase. Droplets of water fell from fissures high above making each step

more treacherous than the last. It also saturated the
walls so that when light reflected off them, they turned
the domelike cavern into a crystalline honeycomb.

As he descended, a distant rumble grew louder and
louder, until the crescendo built to a pulsating roar
that vibrated in the rock beneath his feet, turning his
body into a great tuning fork. At its most extreme
point he stopped, having reached the end of the path,
just above the rushing river of black water that
charged past him to drop into an ominous abyss.

He set his lantern on a protected ledge, sat on a section of waterworn stone, and watched the mist that
rose like countless specters escaping from the rup-
tured bowels of purgatory. Writhing and wrestling they
reached for the safety of his hair, body and clothing,
soon coating him with their phosphorescent tears.

This was his place, the one spot on earth where he
didn't impulsively recoil at the thought of being
touched. He alone could negotiate the perilous path.
He alone knew the mystical shapes that lived here
without light. This was his true home, where he came
to be himself, and to dream.

He needed the mercy of that tonight. The fever was
back, although lately it never seemed to cool. But tonight, especially, it threatened to consume him, and he
felt powerless to fight it.

Oddly enough, he knew what was happening to
him. He was in danger of losing a heart he wasn't
supposed to have. And, oh, the pain of it . . . the tor-
menting, relentless pain.

Throwing back his head, he roared, purging, protesting, praying.

He hadn't asked for this. It was hopeless, useless, a joint mockery conceived by God and devil. He dropped his head, his chin striking his chest.

If only he'd never been born.

Gazing down into the moving water, beyond it, to the entrance to oblivion, he felt the pinch of something fastening on to and tugging at his soul. What a seductive grip. Unfortunately, a greater force kept him rooted where he sat.

Revenge. Sweet, sweet revenge. As it could be. Should be.

The warped ambitions and machinations of a conscienceless man deserved retribution. And he wanted his pound of flesh. More. He wanted the satisfaction of pulverizing his nemesis's very essence into the ground beneath his feet. For years it had been his waking thought, and his continual fantasy. One day, he'd promised himself, he would have that last bit of information he needed to find his human demon.

Reality, however, was intruding.

How could he continue to focus so earnestly, so thoroughly on his dream of being a moral bullet, when *she* kept interfering? He didn't like the way she stirred his conscience with her turn-the-other-cheek philosophy. He owed nothing to no one. If anything on the face of this earth deserved a right to strike back at an injustice, *he* did.

But her presence in these woods was changing him. She was humbling him. Frightening him. Lifting his spirit to some exalted place he didn't belong.

He wanted to curse her for that. She had no right to ask him to be more than science had created. But there was no escaping her. Even here, he could hear her voice.

"What do you believe should matter?"

"I'm trying to understand."

"You aren't getting any better at understanding me at all."

"To me, you'll never be ugly."

No, he didn't have the faintest clue as to what motivated her, especially if her story—or as much of it as he'd let her share thus far—was true, and she'd indeed experienced what she said she had. All he could see was that she was forgiving, tolerant, and kind. In fact her whole persona indicated a quiet state of grace that seemed to reflect a background of privilege and esteem. Thoroughly different from the nightmare she'd briefly described to him.

He wished he could convince himself that she'd been lying. But all his instincts told him that she'd spoken the truth, was in fact a walking testament to the axiom. And that kept luring him back to her.

They were kindred spirits . . . with one critical, hysterical difference. She would find out how much of one if he ever chose to stand before her in broad daylight.

Burning up from the torment, he leaned back against the cool, damp wall and shut his eyes tight to block out the vision of her sweet face. He rubbed his chest to ease the ache within. If he thought it would give him relief, he would gladly claw his fingers and tear out his heart. Despair was growing into a cancer that was slowly killing him.

Paloma . . . Paloma.

"Paloma," he whispered.

Yes. I hear you.

How easy this was becoming. How dangerous. As though nothing more than a sparrow's breath separated them, the connection was made. Too weary, too hungry for a morsel of her gentle spirit, he let it continue.

Forgive me.

There's nothing to forgive.

I go out of my way to hurt you.

You're afraid. I understand. I just wish there was something I could do to help, to assure you that we're no threat to you, as I've tried to explain.

He almost laughed, but it would have been a madman's laugh. No threat? Ah, the deadly innocence of it. Didn't she understand? Now that he knew such a pure heart existed, he was doomed to spend the rest of his life dreaming the useless "if only..." dream. He wanted it. He wanted her.

It's hopeless.

Don't say that! There's always hope. I know. It's what carried me through years of enduring the unspeakable. You must have hope. And faith.

I can't.

You must.

You don't know what you're asking.

I'm giving you choices, not asking.

Yes, you are. In your heart. In your dreams.

He could feel her hesitation, her awe.

Then it is true. There's no barriers between our minds?

Few.

You can read my thoughts at will?

Just as you're reading mine.

And yet you're very far away from me. I can feel it.

It's an unusual phenomenon, yes.

It's a miracle.

It's a curse.

No!

Oh, how he wanted to release himself of this torment. *We must never do this again.*

Why not? If it wasn't for this connection, I would be terrified of you.

Hold onto your fear. Follow its wisdom. It will protect you.

From what?

Me.

No. I'll never be afraid of you again.

The truth of that echoed in his head like the ear-splitting knell of an enormous gong. He gripped his head against the pain.

Oh! I can feel your anguish. Please...what did I say that upset you?

Your blind faith. Your reckless trust. You don't know who... what I am.

It doesn't matter. All that does is that you've been good to us, despite everything. You helped us when we were desperate. You have a good heart. No matter what else you feel you're guilty of, I wouldn't forget that.

He couldn't bear to listen to such things. This merely emphasized how young, how inexperienced she was, and what a romantic to insist on seeing him as a heroic figure.

You don't know what you're saying.

Then tell me—better yet, show me who you are. Come to me. Let me come to you.

Never! Fisting his hands, he used all his strength and concentration to sever the connection between them.

Where did you go? Please. Don't shut me out.

She tried again and again to reunite their minds. But he remained resolute, although he heard everything she said, felt her disappointment and concern for him.

How he yearned to be worthy of such compassion. How he wished he could fulfill her entreaty and his dream, to walk from this self-imposed exile and go to her. How he wished to be a normal, sane, *safe* man.

As he waited, she gave up, finally returning to tuck her animals into bed. Relieved, he let his fatigue have control over his body. He let his imagination begin to paint tempting pictures.

Yes, he could see it. In another time and place, he could see her greeting him at her door, her gentle, dark eyes welcoming, a tender smile curving her mouth.

His heart swelling, he bent and touched his lips to hers for a kiss that, as Marlowe had written, made him immortal. And like in Shelley's *Julian and Maddalo,* he rained kisses on her lips and eyelids, taking pleasure because she believed what she saw.

All he knew about loving he'd learned from the pages of the masters. He'd absorbed enough theory to drive a sane man mad. And himself, for practical experience evaded him. He'd assumed such bliss was out of reach to someone like him. Never did he dream that anyone like *her* might stray so far from safety, and so temptingly close to his grasp.

His thoughts grew bolder. He let himself pretend she led him past the great stove he'd viewed through the windows, past the chairs and cot where her wards slept like contented children, then up the stairs.

How small he imagined her hand felt in his. How soft. He kissed it, and then every finger to show her how precious she was to him. Until she grew flushed. Until her eyes turned bright with longing.

The room she led him to was furnished sparely but was comfortable and clean. At least there was a real bed, he thought, another wave of longing sweeping through him. He'd long craved to know the pleasure of stretching out on down and fresh cotton, of feeling it yielding under his weight, yet welcoming him.

He sucked in a deep breath. His imagination soared. He smelled the clean scent of soap and water, and wildflowers, instead of the cold, musty dampness of this place that had gone too long without experiencing the caress of the sun.

She lit a candle. He stepped behind her and released her hair from its braid, filled his hands with the lustrous wealth that had earned her that blunt but appropriate name from her friends, and lifted the fragrant mass of silk to his face. Then he wrapped his arms around her and drew her back against him. It was heaven, the ecstasy of a lifetime. Nevertheless, three decades of yearning had its own pull.

He let himself be carried by it, visualizing her turning to face him, her gaze serene, trusting. As the reflection of her dreams he had the freedom to kiss her at will, meld their flesh, blend their tastes, impress her soft form on his body.

Soon desire planted new fruits of imagination, stirring him into tense expectancy. Heat coiled in him and he throbbed with the need of relief. Slipping her filmy gown from her shoulders, he saw himself letting it fall to her waist and then bending low to adore the sweet form he'd uncovered.

"Touch me. Love me."

Her voice, the invitation, filled him with new passion and pride. Yes, he would love her. No one would ever bring her the pleasure he would. No one would cherish her more, nor would anyone ever understand better the need to go slow, to be tender, and kind.

Closing his eyes momentarily, he relished the sensations expanding as his blood heated. She would blossom like a spring rose.

Then he opened his eyes and . . .

The shock took his breath away. Something was wrong—dreadfully, horribly wrong.

He looked around the bare, cold, tiled room and frowned. He did not know this place. What's more it had no part in his fantasy. He didn't want to be here, and wished he could rouse fully from this trancelike state.

But the vision went on in spite of his distress.

Get up. Get up and get out. Even as he heard the orders he directed at himself, he realized he was lying on a bed. No . . . not a bed, a table. Yes, it must be a table he thought, eyeing the tiles again. But where? In a hospital? Strange. He didn't feel ill.

Behind him a door opened with the heavy, metallic sound of steel. He tried to twist around to see who was coming, but his head was secured by a strap, as were his arms and legs.

Panic filled him. He didn't like this at all. He shouldn't be here. Didn't want to be here.

And belatedly he smelled the unmistakable scent of death.

With a jerk, he tested the strength of the straps, his heart weighing like lead in his chest. No matter how hard he pulled, the bindings wouldn't give. They were metal. He could break his wrists and ankles and still not free himself.

"There, there, my friend," a low, oddly amiable voice drifted over to him. "There's no need to agitate yourself."

"Let me go. Why am I here?"

"Why shouldn't you be? You belong here. You belong to me."

It didn't make sense, and frightened him greatly. "What are you saying? I'm a free man. Cut me loose or I'll—"

"Do what?"

A not-quite-sane laugh filled the chilly room. He'd heard it before. In his dreams . . . his nightmares . . . at the height of his anger . . . in the depth of his fury.

"Oh, but this is marvelous. You actually see yourself as a man? Then that's a beginning, isn't it? Let's find out what else I achieved with you."

The stranger went to a stainless-steel double sink and proceeded to wash his hands. Then he pulled on a pair of protective gloves.

When he once again faced him, all that was visible was a pair of shrewd eyes the color of cold steel. The rest of his face was hidden by a mask. Even his hair was covered by a cloth cap of blue, the same color of his uniform.

Then the man picked up a slim scalpel.

His blood turned cold. "What are you doing?"

"Why, I'm going to examine you, of course."

"I'm not hurt."

"No. You're an extraordinary specimen, all right. I'm very excited about this."

"Wait!" He cried, as the man again leaned toward him. "You can't do this."

"Why not?"

"I haven't been . . ."

"Anesthetized? Of course not. This is the only way to get a good analysis of how your organs are functioning. Don't worry. Nothing in your genetic background indicates you have refined sensory perceptions. You won't feel much at all."

The lunacy, the horror of that comment left him stunned. But only for seconds. Only until the man slid the scalpel from his chest to his abdomen.

An excruciating pain gripped him, jerking him upright and forward. He lost sense of time and place. Then, suddenly, all he saw before him was black, cold water.

CHAPTER SEVEN

What had that been?

Paloma looked up from her journal, overwhelmed by a feeling of shock and depression. She gazed beyond the geraniums, past her reflection in the kitchen window and out into the dark night, feeling as shaky as if she'd just been jarred out of a nightmare.

Glancing over at the others, she saw they remained fast asleep. Only Old Harry showed signs of actually dreaming; however, his seemed an enjoyable series of images and emotions.

What did that mean? What had she picked up on this time?

It wasn't until the aura of deep anguish continued to press down upon her that she allowed herself to consider a different source, and attempt a connection.

Talk to me.

In the distance an owl hooted, but otherwise the night remained hauntingly silent.

Please. I'm concerned that something's happened. Just let me know that you're not hurt.

It was like asking the table to rise from the floor all by itself. Common sense told her it shouldn't happen. But she believed, and because she believed she expected.

Nothing. Nothing's happened.

She sensed otherwise, but guessed that he would lie outright if necessary to— To what? Keep his dignity? He seemed very proud, and that made her all the more grateful that he'd responded at all. But not certain what to do next, and wondering if she should let the miraculous link between them dissolve again, she decided to tackle his ambivalence head-on.

Go ahead. What is it?

I shouldn't be doing this. Not after I told you it wouldn't happen again.

I'm glad you've changed your mind.

Are you?

Something serious *had* affected him, and whether she wanted it to or not, her heart went out to him. She had spent more than her share of nights awake and afraid to sleep, not to understand the terror the absence of light, or solitude could hold.

I hadn't gone to bed yet. I was working on my journal.

I'm disturbing you.

No! I—I wasn't concentrating very well anyway.

If he wanted to, he wouldn't have to work hard to figure out where her thoughts had been. Paloma wondered if he would try.

What do you write in your journal?

Somewhat disappointed by the question, she forced herself to focus instead on the wariness beneath the curiosity. Tempted or not, he remained suspicious of her every move.

You mustn't worry. You're not in it. I've learned to respect others' privacy too much.

It seems that once again I've misjudged you.

That's all right. It takes time to build trust. As for the journal, it's for Old Harry and the chimps. I keep a log on our daily routine and progress involving primate and human communication, including signing and telepathy. But I also try to explain it more fully with anecdotes and background information.

Paloma realized she was sending out an incredible amount of information that might not be getting through. Feeling extremely foolish, she waited for him to respond, but got nothing.

Did I lose you?

Lose me...? No. You said you were protecting your animals.

I am. I'm trying to. But the abilities and knowledge they possess could help other animals get fairer treatment from the scientific community someday. At least I hope so.

You have doubts.

Like you, I've had my own problems with trust. But Byron, Dr. Metcalf, has been a good friend. I have to believe he'll handle the information I develop for him fairly.

Have to?

Everyone has to take a risk in someone or something sometime.

I hope you're right.

His strong doubt was impossible to miss. Wanting to recapture the chemistry that had existed between them earlier, she thought of something else she could tell him.

I hope you'll believe that you're always welcome here. I'm even working on getting my group to start referring to you as a friend.

That wouldn't be wise.

Why?

Because I am who I am, and that makes all of you vulnerable.

But earlier you admitted—

I also warned you that it can't matter.

He exhausted her with his confusing answers. Unable to stay seated, she rose and walked to the front window. *You hide yourself in ambiguities.*

Consider that a gift.

It doesn't feel like a gift. It's more like an evasion. Even so, I'm glad you changed your mind and reached out to me again. It's not a night to be alone. The stars seem almost within reach. Can you see them from where you are?

No.

From anyone else she supposed the clipped answer would have upset her. But she was beginning to get accustomed to how the more he seemed to care the more abrupt his attitude. Speaking from the heart was best, she decided.

I'm less afraid of the dark when the stars are out, although I prefer the full moon most of all. What can you see? I'm not trying to invade your privacy, I was just wondering.

For a moment she sensed thunder, but a quick look up at the sky told her it was impossible.

I see . . . the edge of oblivion.

No wonder she'd felt he was upset a few moments ago. *It sounds like an intimidating place.*

Every minute of every day is intimidating to me.

Paloma felt another pang of empathy for him. She knew exactly what that was like.

Do you? Really?

It wasn't his skepticism that surprised her, it was his confusion. That most of all took her a moment to recover from and respond.

If there's any way I can help you—ever—I'm here for you.

Although it was a calm night outside, she could have sworn she heard the wind stir. Or was it that he'd sighed?

There is something. You can forgive me for being weak.

She leaned her head against the window's trim. Gazing up at the long river of stars that was part of the Milky Way, she smiled at the incredibility of it, and of his opinion of himself.

Somehow I can't picture you as being weak.

It's best that you don't try to picture me at all.

That just stirs the imagination.

Tell me more about how you became "Hair" to your creatures?

Isn't it obvious? You've seen me.

I've seen you. But I still want to know the story. You tell many, tell me yours. I'm in the mood to hear it tonight.

Lonely, lonely soul. Did he have any idea how much he exposed with a confession like that? And either way, how could she refuse him?

I was twelve. Orphaned. And I came to this dark place. A room. Inside I found Harry, along with others like him. Others who are gone now. That was the day I learned I could communicate without using my voice. It was Harry who showed me, and it was Harry who gave me my animal name.

Your animal name . . . ?

They all have them. Sometimes they call it their secret name. Harry's is Great Jungle Man. That's what orangutan means, you know. He likes the dignity of it. Daisy is known as Kiss Girl because she's always flirting and using her wiles to get herself out of the mischief she's created. Ditto is Shy One. I'm simply Hair because Harry had never seen anything like mine before, and since I was human he was reluctant to romanticize it further. The older I get, the more I appreciate the dilemma he'd faced.

Why do you use your animal name? They rarely use theirs that I've noticed.

True. It's because communicating Paloma, not to mention spelling it through sign, is difficult. But for the most part, animal names are kept secret and only get used in special circumstances. It's one of the apes' ways to retain some independence from humans.

Will they mind that you've told me?

I'm not sure. I suppose it depends what you do with the information.

She'd shared an insight that not even Byron knew about. But it had never occurred to her to keep the information from *him.* That seemed to underscore how much she instinctively trusted him.

I won't break the confidence, Paloma.

Yes, I believe that.

And I can feel your fatigue. You should rest now.

She was tired. Odd how when she relaxed around him, she forgot the weight of the load she was carrying. But she didn't want to end this special exchange. Impulsively, she touched her fingers to the glass.

In a minute. Before I go I want to ask you something. Do you know you haven't told me your name yet?

You know what I'm called.

She almost denied that. Then she recalled the villagers' impulsive designation. She felt ashamed.

No. I won't accept a few individuals' mindless assumptions.

Not even your orangutan's?

If you've heard him, you've heard my responses to them.

For all you know those "responses" as you call them are accurate definitions.

Her head was beginning to throb. *You're putting up walls again.*

Because too much paradise can be as deadly as too little. Sleep in peace, Paloma.

Surprisingly, despite her active mind, she did sleep well. And the next day she worked with more confidence and serenity than she had in ages. The animals seemed to pick up on her mood and that spawned an increased calmness and sense of optimism. They became more communicative than ever, and Paloma found herself relieved when nightfall came, along with their bedtime, to give her a reprieve from her blessings.

The only disappointment was that once again her mysterious visitor confused her by keeping his distance. By the time she climbed into her own bed, she'd done everything from walking the compound perimeter, trying to feel his presence, to focusing intensely in an attempt to recreate a connection. Nothing worked.

By the next morning she managed to be more philosophical about her stranger. She reminded herself that this had happened before, and he'd always reconnected—when he was ready. She supposed she just needed to adapt to his need for space, regardless of how much she, personally, was beginning to crave their impromptu and evocative exchanges.

At any rate, reality demanded its own concentration. That came in the form of their wood supply that needed restocking.

Paloma decided she would collect it herself, while Old Harry, Daisy and Ditto played. If everything seemed as calm and secure as it had been these past few days, then later she would take them with her for the walk deeper into the woods to look for berries.

Old Harry close stay here.

As Paloma exited the front gates, she paused to consider the sober-faced orangutan standing ready to lock her out at the slightest hint of trouble. Crouching down to brush off some dried grass and dirt from the lace on his closed parasol, she nodded.

Hair happy Old Harry watch gate. Hair bring wood. Old Harry, Daisy and Ditto take wood to stack, yes?

Play when Monster dead.

No. No Monster here. Hair say.

She had repeated the same phrase again and again. She had the patience and the determination to repeat it a thousand more times if necessary, until he stopped. Because she believed she spoke the truth.

With a pat on his shoulder, she set out on her way.

After only a few weeks, they'd managed to clean out a significant amount of deadwood in the area, forcing her to search a wider perimeter. It took her several minutes to reach the area she'd last stopped at, then another one or two to decide which direction she would focus on for the day. Then slipping on her gardening gloves to avoid anything that pricked, poisoned or stung, she went to work.

Old Harry greeted her with each delivery. Daisy and Ditto soon became intrigued with the game and also decided to stand watch for her arrivals.

It was sometime after she'd set out on her fourth or fifth trip that she sensed a change in the woods. The songbirds, everything, suddenly went silent. The squirrels raced for cover. With the hairs on her arms rising, she too, went still and listened . . . because the sensations were all wrong. Different.

There. To her right. In the thick batch of evergreen shrubbery, she saw a movement between the branches. It crouched low, like something stalking, or preparing to pounce. Bigger than a dog, smaller than a man, Paloma's imagination raced at the thought of what it could be.

Just as she decided that staying absolutely still would be the best course of action, the figure came around the edge of the brush. Rifle barrel first, then smooth hand and plaid-shirt-covered arm. Finally she looked into the round-cheeked face of a young man no older than she. Paloma was too incensed to be relieved.

"How dare you!"

With a strangled gasp as he spotted her for the first time, he backed up a step, and she found herself looking down the bore of his weapon. Not the wisest thing she'd ever done, she decided, belatedly noticing how he was shaking worse than someone with a fever. At the same time, she couldn't believe his nerve.

"What do you mean by poaching in these woods?"

"But I'm not—"

"It's not even close to hunting season," she snapped before he could finish. Never mind that she didn't know when any of the seasons began. "So don't think about using that excuse."

"Lady, ma'am, I'm not hunting. I'm only looking for my goat."

"Your what?"

"I lost my goat."

Paloma pushed up the sleeves of the college T-shirt Byron had given her, and placed her fists on her hips. Now she'd heard everything. She'd never had much contact with a goat before, but they were miles from town. What would a goat be doing way out here?

"I swear," the sallow-faced trespasser replied, as he abruptly redirected his rifle barrel to the ground. "It chewed through its rope a couple days ago, and I've been tracking it ever since."

"Have you? You look more like you're ready to unload your gun into anything that moves," she muttered with a nod toward his weapon.

At least he had the grace to look embarrassed. "Guess you got me jumpy. I thought you might be . . . well, you know."

"No, tell me."

"It."

"*It?*"

"The thing that's running these woods and killing our livestock. You must've heard? Are you the lady staying at the old Sims place?"

Ignoring the queasy feeling the question gave her, Paloma lifted her chin and met his gaze directly. "Yes. I live there. But I haven't seen anything like what you've described."

"Consider yourself lucky. I don't know how you do it, staying out here by yourself." His saucer-round eyes darted from bush, to tree, to shadow.

"I manage just fine, thank you."

This was what she'd been dreading since moving up here—the accidental intrusions, and those from the curious, and the so-called well-intentioned. Next they would see her working with her animals and ask questions, spread rumors.... What if someone from the press got a bright idea to do a feature on her? What if it was picked up by various news services? Isaac didn't watch television often, but he rarely missed the news.

"Anyway, you're the one I come to see."

"Excuse—" She must have missed something. "Me? Why?"

"To ask that if you spot Gulliver, you send him home. He's getting on in years and he's blind in one eye. My dad says he should have been sold for dog food a long time ago so he could get some of his investment back."

Paloma shoved her hands into her jeans' pockets and struggled to keep her temper. His father sounded like someone who deserved to be condemned to a diet of dog food for the rest of his life.

"But I couldn't do that to Gulliver. He was my first 4-H animal. I'd feel like a murderer."

It was too crazy a story not to be true, especially since the young man looked ready to cry. What's more, Paloma felt truly sorry for the creature if it had wandered into the woods and got lost. But she couldn't have this person stomping around with a dangerous weapon.

"As I said before," she told him firmly, "I haven't seen your goat, but I'd be willing to take your address. If I find him, I'll bring him to you."

He fumbled in his pockets and took out one of his father's business cards. It turned out that he was Harold Westman's son. Mr. Westman owned the drugstore where Paloma had shopped for first-aid supplies.

"I'm Douglas," he added.

"All right," she said, pocketing the card. "I'll see what I can do. Now you'd better get on back to town before you hurt someone with that thing."

She watched him head for the road. He seemed eager to be on his way. Nevertheless, she waited until she could no longer hear the sound of his footsteps. Until the birds started talking again. Until all the animals returned. Then she waited a while longer, just in case it had all been a lie, and he'd decided to backtrack to try to sneak into the compound. A part of her admitted she was getting paranoid, but better safe than sorry, she told herself.

Finally, she allowed herself to relax and she started collecting another armload of wood. This time she took a little more time to look for footprints, anything that might indicate there had been a different type of hooved animal in the area. Of course, that proved almost humorous, since she couldn't tell a deer hoof from a goat's.

That struck a memory. Maybe she had seen Douglas Westman's pet, she thought, remembering the day of the storm. But that had been miles away. Surely the animal hadn't wandered this far north?

Ten minutes passed, or perhaps twenty. She lost track of time, especially when she succeeded in locating a set of prints that piqued her interest, and her guilt.

She couldn't ignore it. Her gaze focused on the ground, she felt like a bloodhound. But she followed the meandering path, so rapt in her discovery that she forgot about looking for additional firewood.

Suddenly, she hit a proverbial brick wall in the form of a thicket of spruce. The armload of wood she'd been clinging to slipped. No amount of frantic jockeying could reposition the mass. At the same instant the whole pile began tumbling to the ground, she heard the scream.

Brief, terrible and unmistakable, it cut through the bright early morning like the most awful of nightmares. Abandoning her wood, she clapped her hands over her ears, her memory shooting into overdrive. Images flashed in her eyes, pictures of other times, darker places, and cruel deaths.

No, she thought, and without thinking of her own safety she ran to offer what help she could.

The sound had come from the other side of the trees, and to the right. She headed that way and found another trail almost immediately. Recognized it. It led to the stream. The busy place where all the forest creatures converged periodically during the day and night to drink. Innocently, they would lower their heads to the water, wanting only to slake their thirst, aware of how such a need made them vulnerable.

She ran as fast as she could, and called herself various forms of a fool as she slapped one branch after another out of her way. She knew she took too many risks. Always. One of these days, she told herself, she was going to get hurt. But she didn't let the thought slow her down.

Determined, she barged her way through a particularly thick barrier of brush. Emerging on the other side, she came upon a scene that her mind immediately told her was impossible, and reared back as the crouching creature spun around and roared at her.

"Oh, my God!" she gasped, and turned her back on a horror already imprinted in her memory.

NO RISK, NO OBLIGATION TO BUY...NOW OR EVER!

GUARANTEED

PLAY "ROLL A DOUBLE" AND GET AS MANY AS FIVE FREE GIFTS!

HERE'S HOW TO PLAY:

1. Peel off label from front cover. Place it in space provided at right. With a coin, carefully scratch off the silver dice. This makes you eligible to receive two or more free books, and possibly another gift, depending on what is revealed beneath the scratch-off area.

2. Send back this card and you'll receive brand-new Silhouette Shadows™ novels. These books have a cover price of $3.50 each, but they are yours to keep absolutely free.

3. There's no catch. You're under no obligation to buy anything. We charge nothing – ZERO – for your first shipment. And you don't have to make any minimum number of purchases – not even one!

4. The fact is thousands of readers enjoy receiving books by mail from the Silhouette Reader Service™ months before they're available in stores. They like the convenience of home delivery and they love our discount prices!

5. We hope that after receiving your free books you'll want to remain a subscriber. But the choice is yours – to continue or cancel, anytime at all! So why not take us up on our invitation, with no risk of any kind. You'll be glad you did!

You'll look like a million dollars when you wear this lovely necklace! Its cobra-link chain is a generous 18" long, and the multi-faceted Austrian crystal sparkles like a diamond!

NOT ACTUAL SIZE

"ROLL A DOUBLE!"

PLACE LABEL HERE

SCRATCH HERE

?

SEE CLAIM CHART BELOW

200 CIS ALAZ
(U-SIL-SH-12/93)

YES! I have placed my label from the front cover into the space provided above and scratched off the silver dice. Please rush me the free books and gift that I am entitled to. I understand that I am under no obligation to purchase any books, as explained on the back and on the opposite page.

NAME _____

ADDRESS _____ APT. _____

CITY _____ STATE _____ ZIP CODE _____

CLAIM CHART

🎲 🎲	**4 FREE BOOKS PLUS FREE CRYSTAL PENDANT NECKLACE**
🎲 🎲	**3 FREE BOOKS**
🎲 🎲	**2 FREE BOOKS**

CLAIM NO.37-829

THE SILHOUETTE READER SERVICE™: HERE'S HOW IT WORKS

CHAPTER EIGHT

Only a few yards behind her lay a felled deer, the animal she knew she'd heard crying out as it had met its violent death. She stared at the mottled palette of greenery before her and saw instead how the victim lay opened from throat to belly, its blood all over its killer's hands and face.

His face.

It was him, she knew it. For an instant she'd seen something in his eyes, that flicker of knowledge that said all the illusions and evasions were over. It was him.

Only what was he?

Like being caught on a merry-go-round gone out of control, Paloma watched every moment of the last few weeks flash before her eyes, as she waited her own brutal end. Oh, yes, she knew it now—all the signs building to this moment had been there. He'd warned her, too. Tried to help her, in his own way. The roar at her front door. The episode by the berry thicket. The one when the tree fell on Ditto. So many warnings. But like some deaf, dumb and blind fool, she'd focused on the idealistic, the romantic. She'd chosen only to see his humanness.

No one can help me.

You disturb me.

Words flow from your lips and torment my soul . . . my soul . . . my soul.

Each one of those admissions had been another chip at her ability to stay emotionally distant and responsible. The most damning words, however, had been her own promise to him.

To me, you'll never be ugly.

Slowly, she turned back to face him. A low sound, a sound of excruciating pain, rumbled in his throat, then he tried to avoid her gaze.

"Go from here," he commanded heavily. "Do not look on this."

Not pain, she amended, suddenly understanding. Something far less corrigible. Grief. Shame. She could feel it swelling and festering in him like a malignancy.

Tears began to sting in her eyes, but she willed them away. Clenching her hands into fists, and steeling her spine, she took a deep breath, forcing down revulsion and fear. "Wash up in the stream," she managed to tell him through numb lips. "I'll wait."

For a moment she wondered if he might not refuse. The way he stared at her, she thought he might. His eyes were the same crystalline-blue ones she'd seen in her dreams, cunning, shrewd. They could easily belong to a wolf judging its next prey. Then he released her from their mesmerizing hold by silently doing as she'd directed.

As he rose to his feet, her breath was almost pulled from her lungs again. She'd never seen anyone so tall and powerfully built. He was a massive being, standing easily a head and shoulders above her, and those shoulders . . . there were few trees in these woods that could match their width.

How strange, she thought, battling a new wave of dizziness, after those two distinctive features, it became virtually impossible to describe him. What she could determine was that while beneath his crude leather clothing he had the silhouette of a man... genetically he was far more. Or less.

She could see potentially several orders of beast. His eyes suggested one, the wild mane of midnight-black hair that virtually covered his body, was another, his clawed fingers yet a third....

The heart-wrenching truth, she realized swallowing hard, was that what had happened to him couldn't have been an accident of nature. The terrifying truth was that it had to mean there was more than one Dr. Isaac Tredway operating unpoliced in the world. The thought sent a shiver through her unlike any she'd ever experienced.

As the stream carried away the last of the deer's blood, he rose, his movements reflecting a breathtaking, enviable grace. But rather than face her, he stayed partially turned away, and instead of meeting her gaze, he concentrated on the moss-covered rock to her right.

"I've never been more ashamed of what I am than at this moment," he whispered hoarsely.

The pain in her chest was hardly bearable. Could a heart actually rend itself in two from grief? Helpless not to, she pressed a hand to her chest and once again forced herself to consider the body between them. Unbidden came a memory, an important one. She recalled his warning about his need for flesh.

Understanding in a wholly new way, she bowed her head. "You can't help being who you are."

"*What* I am."

Stung by his bitterness, she winced. How could she judge him? He was already doing a lethal job torturing himself. She couldn't begin to imagine how he'd managed to carry the burden he had for all these years. The fact that he existed at all was a miracle, if a brutal one.

"How did this happen?" she asked, hoping he would forgive her need to comprehend.

"What does it matter? The point is that it did...and I survived."

Yes, he had. She wondered if he understood what that meant. "You have great courage."

Bewildered, he shot her a quick look. But just as swiftly he withdrew his gaze, as though he believed the very impudence of it might offend her.

"Except for my mother," he began, his voice thick and his words reluctant, "you're the only person who's ever looked at me and not been repulsed. Even the lowliest creature in these woods avoids me with dread."

His mother. Paloma wondered about the woman who'd carried him in her womb. Who had she been? Or—another quick stab of pain gripped her anew—what?

"She was a woman not unlike yourself."

He spoke gently and it humbled her. She didn't deserve such generosity, not when she'd neglected to remember their strong mental link that would expose him to her careless thoughts.

"I'm sorry. I meant no disrespect. This is simply all so..."

"I understand." He bent and picked up his kill, slinging it over his shoulder as though it was nothing heavier than a sack of duck down.

Realizing he intended to leave, she cried, "Wait!"

He hesitated, but kept his back to her, and Paloma clasped her hands together, unsure what she'd meant to say or had a right to ask. She only knew she couldn't let him go away like this.

She could feel his despondency as if it were her own. Regardless of what he'd been forced to do for his survival, the link between them had grown stronger. That made her intrepid.

Taking a step closer, she murmured, "You have to tell me. Your mother . . . what did she name you?"

At first she thought he might not reply, she could tell by the sudden rigidity in his body, and felt it in his inner turmoil. But just as she decided to tell him that it didn't matter, she could sense him yielding to her.

"She didn't name me."

Paloma winced and had to fight the strongest impulse to touch him, stroke his back. What had she been thinking? Of course the poor soul hadn't named him; in all probability the woman hadn't even survived the birth. Hadn't she been forced to watch a primate mother die because of what Isaac had implanted in her?

"I shouldn't have asked."

"No, you misunderstand. She didn't name me because once she realized I would live, she decided I should name myself."

Her mouth dry, her eyes burning, Paloma slowly circled him, until she could once again look up into his face. Although he immediately averted his own gaze, she cautiously reached up and wiped away the trace of blood that remained at the corner of his mouth.

A soft, barely perceptible growl rose from deep within him, the reflex of a wild beast who didn't know whose touch would be kind and whose would be cruel. But his eyes . . . his shocked, pained stare gave her the courage to believe she'd reached through to the man deep inside.

"And what did you choose?" she asked gently.

"Dunndrogo."

Clearly unprepared to have exposed so much to her, he sidestepped her. Then, without another word, he walked away, disappearing into the dense brush.

What had he done? *What had he done?*

The question pounded in Dunndrogo's head, as he hurried through the woods. Furious with himself, and grappling with an unnamed fear, he took no pleasure in the fact that having taken nourishment, his strength had been revived. All he could focus on were his errors.

He'd made the mistake of a lifetime—and to be seen at his most base, most vulnerable state! Once again he shuddered with shame, and it turned the lingering sweetness in his mouth to bile. He wanted nothing more than to retreat to a dark corner somewhere and suffer in blessed isolation. But such a luxury could not be his, at least not yet. First he needed to deliver his prey and confess his breach.

At the point where the woods ended abruptly and the rocks jutted from the earth like an army of angry fists, he paused to glance back and listen. No, she hadn't made the mistake of following him, as he feared she might. He sensed nothing close by.

Grimly, he climbed, feeling the sun burning his quarry's blood into his tunic. He needed to bathe. His craving to wash off all traces of this particular kill as soon as possible was almost desperate. What's more, he knew he couldn't accept any clothing made from this creature's hide. It would spawn too many memories. Not that he was likely to forget this day.

He entered the cave. The darkness would have been a relief, if he'd been alone. But *she* stood at the table sharpening her knife, and her smile of welcome only served to inspire another pang of conscience.

"At last! Oh, it's a beauty. You've done well."

Her blue-gray eyes sparkled with a rarely seen pleasure. It took years off her deeply lined face. But Dunndrogo wouldn't allow himself to bask in her relief and happiness. He simply deposited his load on the solidly built table and stood back to give her room to inspect it.

"Yes, marvelous. There's enough here to make a fine tunic for you." After stroking the soft pelt, she inspected the carcass's immaculately cleaned torso cavity. "Have you eaten?"

"Yes."

Something in his tone must have gotten through to her. She stopped her inspection and turned to him.

"What is it? What's wrong?"

"Something happened after the kill. I suppose it was the creature's cry."

"Someone came? You were *seen*?"

"There was no avoiding it."

She lifted her hand to her mouth. "I told you this would happen. Didn't I warn you?" The fanned fingers clenched into a fist. "How could you be so careless?"

Dunndrogo stood silent and lowered his gaze to the floor, willing to take her anger because, somehow, his own disgust with himself hardly seemed adequate punishment. Secretly, however, his thoughts drifted.

He envisioned Paloma, and remembered with an aching poignancy the compassion in her dark eyes and the tenderness of her childlike fingers when she'd touched him. He would gladly suffer any forfeit, including death, than to have missed that singular sensation.

"Well, what's done is done. There's nothing to do but get rid of her."

That won his attention fast. "You can't be serious?"

"She's dangerous. She can only bring you, *us*, trouble. She must be dealt with."

He couldn't believe what he was hearing. "Exactly what do you mean by 'dealt with'?"

She busied herself by wiping her hands on her worn, stained apron. "Isn't it obvious?"

"You'd condone the murder of an innocent woman? She's barely begun her life!"

"I'm not without sympathy for her, but as you've been forced to accept yourself, necessity makes its own rules. Knowing what she does, she can't very well be let free to do heaven only knows what damage. For all you know, she's already left to spread the word."

It struck him that *that* thought hadn't even entered his mind. The realization told him all he needed to know about how deep the taproots of his feelings for her had grown.

"I think you're being too hasty with your conclusions," he replied slowly. He needed to be careful about how much he exposed. He needed time to think. "After observing her these last weeks, I believe she's not the type of person to cause trouble."

"Hmph. How did she act when she saw you?"

New suspicion and unmistakable disapproval narrowed her eyes and pinched her lips. Dunndrogo saw that it would be useless to evade the truth, and decided not to try.

"She accepted me."

"You're not serious?"

"I say she did."

"You mean she pretended to. My God," she groaned, shaking her head, "she must be more cunning than I imagined."

"No!" He couldn't let Paloma be so maligned. Somehow it seemed almost criminal. "You haven't met her. You don't know. Initially, she was shocked, of course," he explained, trying to choose his words carefully. "But afterward, she was . . . She has a great capacity for compassion and kindness."

"My poor, sweet fool. This paragon you're describing will bring catastrophe upon us. Mark my words."

"I've never let harm come near you, and I don't deserve your lack of faith now," Dunndrogo ground out. Neither able nor willing to stand and listen to any more, he wheeled away, and headed up the slope.

"Where are you going?"

"To search for an hour of peace. It's obvious there's none for me here."

Hair go. Old Harry go.

Paloma bent from the waist and rested her hands on her knees to nuzzle the four-foot-tall orangutan. He rarely looked so concerned for her safety, which meant she must have come back from her last excursion into the woods looking more upset than she'd imagined.

Old Harry stay. Hair think good idea.

Hair go berries get?

She shook her head. That option definitely had to be tabled considering what had already happened this morning. In fact, they would have to postpone any such excursions for a while.

No wood?

Again she shook her head. She'd found them an adequate supply for the time being. But how did she tell him that she felt the strongest urge to go back to see if she could find that rambunctious goat? Harry had no idea what a goat was, anyway. What's more, she didn't have any great hope of finding it; she only knew she had to try.

Home soon. Lock gate.

With a parting kiss to the top of his head, she hurried out of the compound.

It was difficult to walk away. She kept picking up on his telepathic messages, his entreaties, for a considerable distance, even after a glance back told her the vegetation oblitered his view of her from the compound. She hoped he would soon accept this impulsive excursion, and find something to do to entertain himself until she got back. The girls seemed to have dealt with this change in their routine well enough. Then again, they approved of anything that kept them from having to concentrate on lessons.

The unusual silence she'd noticed before continued to permeate the woods. The farther she walked, the more pronounced it became. Paloma wondered if it was a result of Dunndrogo's successful hunt, or perhaps he'd only wanted her to think he'd left. The latter thought kicked her heartbeat into overdrive, forcing her to admit to herself that she wasn't only going out to search for Douglas Westman's pet; secretly, she had hopes of meeting Dunndrogo again, too.

Dunndrogo. Such a mysterious, exotic name. What did it mean? How had he chosen it? *How* had he survived this long without anyone knowing he existed? Well, they knew, she amended, but only that something strange was going on in their woods; however, as far as she knew no one had ever actually seen him.

Her heart went out to him for all he must have suffered over the years. She wanted to make sure he understood that. She needed to ask him questions, too. Before, when she'd come upon him at that place, the horrible scene had been too overwhelming for words. She'd recovered somewhat, and there were things she had to have explained.

With barely a clue about where to look, she had no option but to rely on her telepathic abilities, in the hopes that he would respond to her. When that didn't work, she explored the spot where she'd last seen him, trying hard not to look at the dark stain on the grass. Then her search took her to the berry patch. But once again her efforts were unsuccessful.

Maybe she'd try a little farther, she thought, as she looked upstream where a narrower path ran alongside it. She wondered where it led. Could it go to someplace special he'd found for himself? That would explain why he'd been so good at disappearing for days at a time. Yielding to a hunch, she started down the trail.

After venturing maybe a quarter of a mile, she felt him. The sensation came like a marble headstone falling upon her chest. She had to stop and catch her breath, his state of oppression was so great.

Finally, easing her way around a few more bushes, she came to a picturesque cove, and the end of her search.

He sat hunched over a lovely pool of calm water, gazing at his reflection. Although his hair hid him, she knew what his expression reflected: despair over the face he saw in the mirrorlike water, and a deep-seated need to understand *why* fate had chosen this burden for him.

"That's no more help than looking for answers in a crystal ball," she told him.

For a moment she didn't think he would answer, but he surprised her by murmuring, "I should have known you'd find me."

"It wasn't that difficult. I felt the weight of your burden, and your turmoil." Paloma edged nearer and eased down beside him on a patch of lush green grass near the bank. She considered his reflection, and then his profile. "What can I do to help?"

"Nothing. Nothing can be done."

"You sound...defeated."

"Perhaps I am."

"No. Not you. Never *you*."

He shot her a strange, brief look. Then, as though relentlessly aware of his own visage, he averted his face. "Why do you ignore your fear and seek me out?"

"That's not an easy question to answer."

"Try. It's important."

She thought about the shock and revulsion she'd felt when she'd initially recoiled from the tragedy downstream. She thought of her shame afterward, over what she'd belatedly realized he could not help. How did she communicate that, despite everything, she couldn't help but trust him?

The soft expulsion of breath had her turning back to him. That's when she realized explanations were unnecessary. Once again he'd read—not only her thoughts, but her heart.

He exhaled as though overcome. Staring at his reflection, he murmured, "It wasn't until I could read that I named myself. Books were my universe, but I didn't know to think that as odd because I didn't know that I was... different. Not for years. I'd been carefully insulated from the world that was waiting to prove ready, willing and able to show me otherwise. There were no mirrors where I resided. I didn't even know what the word mirror meant, until I came upon it in a book."

"And so you went to find one, didn't you?" Paloma said, feeling the strain behind his attempt to sound indifferent.

"Yes. But I was unsuccessful. And then I found this," he replied, reaching down to touch his fingers to the surface. The wake of fine ripples created a kaleidoscope of his image. "Would you believe, I jumped in? Like the fool I was, I tried to fight the image, as though something could be done."

Paloma bit back the sound of protest that rose to her lips. "Someone should have eased you toward this."

"Someone tried. It couldn't be helped that I had an impatient, uncontrollable mind." He drew in a deep breath. "Not long after that, I named myself Dunndrogo. I took the words from an old book, dunn standing for dark, and drogo for ghost. It suits me, don't you think?"

She ignored his sarcasm and answered from the heart. "It's a beautiful, noble name."

He looked doubtful at first, and then hopeful. "Truly?" Just as quickly he retreated behind his remoteness and pretended it didn't matter. "I spent the next several years of my life reading everything I could get my hands on. Even if I had to steal a book to do so," he said as though challenging her to criticize him for it.

Paloma knew what he was doing. He wanted to know if her value system would judge him as a thief for what society had forced him to do, and if society's law superseded a moral law. She had no answers, or at least knew she was the wrong person to entertain the question, since she'd broken enough of her own.

"I hope that at least you read well," she said with a lopsided smile.

"From someone called H. G. Wells I read *The Outline Of History*. Thomas Jefferson taught me ethics. Thoreau, values. I greatly admired his *Walden*."

"Many people have," Paloma murmured, remembering her own personal connection with the works. "He was a Harvard graduate, and yet he became one of the great mystics of his age. Did you know that?"

"What's Harvard?"

Paloma couldn't help but grin at that. "A college. For most people those are places you go where they tell you what to think as opposed to how to think." It was an irreverent response, but she wasn't at all sorry for it. After all, such a place had created Dr. Isaac Tredway and countless others like him.

He took a moment to consider her words, then murmured, "I suppose he did better as the mystic then, didn't he?"

"Without a doubt." Paloma chuckled, enjoying this sharing. "Dunndrogo," she said, tasting the name again, "will you tell me how you came to—"

"No."

So much for lowering barriers. It seemed they were back to old rules. "You know I will keep your secret."

He shifted to sit with his back to the water, but concentrated on the grass between his feet, rather than meeting her searching gaze. For the first time Paloma noticed he wore moccasinlike slippers coarsely made out of some type of hide.

"I know you would," he replied on a sigh. "But this cannot go on."

"What can't?"

He seesawed his hand between them. "This...giving parts of ourselves to each other. The connection between us is growing too strong."

She couldn't believe he wanted to denounce it now. Before, yes. But now that she'd seen him and could accept who he was? "You've known we had this special closeness all along."

"I was wrong to let it go as far as it did. Now I must stop it!"

"Then all you have to do is never come near us again. Or open your thoughts to me," she added quietly.

Restless, frustrated, he turned farther away. "I knew this would happen. From the beginning it's been a straight road toward catastrophe."

"Meaning what?"

"Stop calling me to you." Although he met her direct stare, he looked momentarily surprised at his own violence. "It must end. Here. Now. Or we'll destroy each other."

Paloma couldn't believe what she was hearing. Admittedly theirs was a strange friendship, but not when she considered how they'd each come from unorthodox backgrounds. How could he cast that aside?

"You're breaking my heart," she whispered.

She thought nothing could touch her so deeply again. The loss of her mother only weeks after childbirth was simply a story her father had once explained to her. Losing her father had been difficult, yes; but she'd only been a child, and soon her adoptive uncle's experiments had obliterated all self-pity from her mind.

But if Dunndrogo removed himself from her life, he would leave behind a cavity that nothing would ever fill again. Didn't he realize that?

"You mustn't think that way," he said, reading her mind again. "*I* mustn't."

She could only shake her head. Never would she accept what he was asking.

He pressed forward. "Look at me!" he ground out. "See me for what I *am*."

"I have looked." Although she managed to keep her eyes dry, she was unable to stop the tears from thickening her voice. "And what I see is one of the most magnificent beings God ever created."

With a groan, Dunndrogo pushed himself to his feet. "No god created me, a devil did!"

Paloma couldn't argue against that deduction. After all, she'd spent her childhood in the hands of one herself. But it wasn't a devil that inspired his spirit. And it wasn't a devil who she'd been addressing, or who'd been speaking to her all these weeks. Most of all, it wasn't a devil who was trying to protect her now.

"Don't let yourself believe that," he said, having again clearly accessed her mind. "You must learn not to be too brave. Don't trust me too much. I've killed, Paloma. And not just for food."

Despite the jolt that gave her heart, Paloma forced herself to ask, "What do you mean, not just for food?"

He paced restlessly from an ancient spruce tipping toward the water, to her, then back again, finally gripping the tree's bowed trunk as though needing its support. "Years ago my mother did what I do now to get supplies. It was late as she made her way back to the woods, and she came face-to-face with a poacher hunting by flashlight. He thought she was a deer coming through the brush."

"Oh, no," Paloma whispered.

"It was an easy conclusion to draw, considering she'd made her clothes out of deerskin as often as not."

"He shot her?"

"Yes. I was nearby when I heard the rifle go off, and although she'd always instructed me to stay hidden no matter what happened, I raced to help her." He let his head fall to his chest. "Something happened to me that had never happened before. I lost control. I became a creature of violence."

"You were protecting your mother."

"Perhaps. Initially. I know that if I hadn't been as fast as I was, he would have gotten off a second, more accurate shot. But the point is that I couldn't have stopped my blind rage if I'd wanted to. And I didn't want to."

Dear God. "Dunndrogo, did she—"

"Do not ask me that."

His harsh response silenced her for several moments. That wasn't unwelcome. Realizing this was the story she'd heard in the village about how one of their residents had been mauled by a wild animal, Paloma needed a moment to recover.

Rising, she paced the width of the small area. No, somehow she had to make him see that anyone in such a state would have had a similar impulse to defend a loved one.

"You're suggesting that only animals kill recklessly and that's not true. I've studied this, Dunndrogo. Byron has shared many reports with me. Animals have built-in inhibitions toward violence just like humans do. In fact maybe more because emotionally it's far more difficult to kill with your bare hands than it is to express violence with a gun. Oh, please listen to me," she cried, taking hold of his arm and pressing her forehead to his water-soaked back.

With a harsh growl, he swung around and thrust her away from him. The force of his move sent her flying and she landed in the briars lining the path.

Incredulous, Paloma stared at him, and then the blood beginning to run across her palm.

CHAPTER NINE

Although the sight of her bleeding hand filled him with self-loathing, and the return of uncertainty in her eyes almost destroyed him, Dunndrogo forced himself to maintain his threatening demeanor.

"I am *this*," he growled down at her. "Don't try to mold me into one of your tamed creatures. It could cost you everything."

He stalked away, fighting the desperation that urged him to rush back, to take her into his arms, and hold her close to his heart. It also cost him considerable concentration to lock her out of his mind, when she tried to draw him back. He knew he had to be brutal in order for her to believe, no, to *understand* that he was capable of anything.

As he was.

As he would always be, he reminded himself, during his trek back to the cave.

Upon his arrival, he wasn't surprised to find that work had gone on without him. The processing of their food wasn't something he ordinarily involved himself with, unless the animal's weight was overwhelming or the skinning awkward. That hadn't been the case this time.

The deer had already been skinned. Its hide was now being stretched on the frame built from material he'd obtained in the village. He'd designed it following a picture in a book on North American Indians.

The carcass lay on the table, ready for the meat to be stripped from the bone. Most of it would be laid out in long thin slices. After a heavy salting, the meat would be left to dry for several days. Eventually, it would be stored in a barrel in the next chamber, a place almost as cold as the refrigerators he'd once learned about in the village.

First, however, one roast would be cut from the hindquarter, and cooked on the spit for tonight's feast. Although instinctively he craved his meat raw, and rarely touched the salted portions, occasionally he enjoyed the taste, as well as the companionship a cooked meal provided.

Later, when the processing was done, it would be his responsibility to carry all the bones and scraps to another part of the woods, a considerable distance northwest of the area. That's where the hungry scavengers he'd frightened away from this location knew to look for his offering. Finally, squirrels and rodents would feast on the bones, concluding nature's cycle. He thought it a far more efficient process, and respectful one, than the one the villagers maintained with their ugly, unhealthy landfill projects.

"From the look on your face, I suppose you've dealt with things?"

She'd barely spared him a glance so far, but the tender gruffness with which she spoke told Dunndrogo that she wasn't without sympathy, regardless of what she'd been expecting of him. It didn't make him feel any better. The fact remained, she wasn't going to be pleased with what he had to tell her.

"You have, haven't you?"

"In my own way. As I told you before that I would."

Finished with the securing of the hide, she turned to him. After a long studious look, she threw up her bloodied hands in a familiar gesture of frustration, before returning to the table. "I should have known," she muttered. "It's been years since your head was turned by a pretty face. I suppose it was just a matter of time before it happened again."

Dunndrogo could have clarified something about that, but kept the information to himself. "She won't pose any future danger to us," he told her instead.

"How can you be sure?"

Because as Paloma had said herself, he'd done his best to break her heart. Worse, because he'd been physically cruel, and if there was one thing that his insight into Paloma's consciousness had shown him, it was that she could not allow herself to accept physical force. By anyone.

This, too, he kept to himself, and only replied, "When have we been certain of anything?"

In anticipation of the lecture he knew to expect, he circled her to add wood to the fire. If he could keep his hands and part of his mind preoccupied, he might not be as deeply affected.

"I need more reassurances than that," she began, a warning in her voice.

"There aren't any to give. We can only take one day at a time."

"And what if your hunch about her is wrong?" she flung at his back.

Dunndrogo added kindling to the warm coals in the middle of the pyre, then stacked a few larger pieces of wood over them. He frowned at the orange-red glow that immediately began devouring the thin wood chips. Survival of the fittest, he thought, that was the lesson nature taught him again and again. Exceptions were rare, out of necessity.

"If it is," he muttered, "we'll deal with it then."

"You're looking extremely pale."

Paloma knew it, and the fact that it was now July and the weather had been absolutely glorious lately gave her few explanations to offer Byron, not to mention excuses. This was his first visit in two weeks, due to some unexpected and demanding study hours at work, he'd explained. It was only natural for him to be more observant than usual.

"I've been working in the house, trying to make more of the rooms useful," she said, feeling comfortable with the answer because it was true enough. It simply wasn't the only truth. "Come on, I'll show you."

She had been cleaning, and painting in one of the downstairs rooms. It had come to her to build the chimps an indoor gym of sorts, for when the harsh winter weather made it impossible to go outside. She'd discarded the trash that had been lying around, and the walls had needed a new base coat of paint. In the midst of that chore, she decided to try her hand at mural painting, in the hope of turning the bland square of space into a tropical forest of sorts.

As she led Byron into the room, she eyed the dozens and dozens of trees and ferns she'd painted in every hue of green she could mix together from the modest offerings she'd found at the village hardware store. The parrots and the flowers she'd added for color diversity made her smile go somewhat lopsided. The project had been a feat, what with the chimps begging for their own paintbrushes. Considering the final results, she had a feeling they could have done a more skillful job.

"Since the ceilings are wonderfully high in these old houses, I'm going to get them a mini-trampoline I saw at the general store in town. And there's this wooden jungle gym set in a magazine that I think I can copy and build myself without too much trouble. What do you think?"

"It's . . . colorful."

His wide-eyed, slightly glazed expression told her more. "You think it's awful."

"No! I just . . . what if you can't stay, Paloma? What if tomorrow Isaac comes barreling in through those gates?"

"Then we'll run. If there's time," she added, careful to keep her tone somber because she didn't want him to think she wasn't taking his warning seriously.

"But all this work will have been a waste. And who knows? Isaac might even file charges against you for trespassing and damaging his private property."

Why was he suddenly sounding like a sand snail? "Byron, all of life is a gamble. If there's anything your experience with me has proven, it's that. The chimps are still *babies*. They need to have fun, and exercise. They didn't know the meaning of the word during their first year in the lab. Thanks to you, they learned quickly at your farm. But this is colder country. I have to adjust where I can. If my efforts last only a few months...then so be it. It will be the best few months of their lives."

"You're right," he muttered. Drawing a deep breath, he placed his hands on his trim hips, and turned around and around, nodding all the while. "I'll see what I can do to find you a small swing-set frame. We'll get some strapping material like what professional movers use, and add a set of rings to what you have in mind."

"Then you don't think it's a silly idea?"

"No. Sweet. Generous. But not silly. And you're right that the winter will prove a challenge for all of you. Plus, don't forget I warned you that the older the girls get, the more rambunctious they're bound to become. As a rule, chimps' personalities change a great deal as they mature."

She remembered his lectures and the case studies he'd made her read. She also remembered how careful Isaac had been with handling the sexually mature specimens. Some were so violent he even had them in collars and strapped to leashes inside their cages. Thankfully those, she remembered with a shiver, never survived long.

"I'll never cage my animals, Byron."

"And if one bites you?"

He never let her forget the studies going back as far as Dr. Albert Schweitzer's experiences in Gabon with the potent virus apes carried. Specifically, the frightening RNA, or retrovirus, that scientists learned could change according to its host and thereby escape destruction by the immune system. Because it attacked the nerves, death promised to be painful and certain.

Oh, yes, she believed in having a healthy respect for caution. But she also knew whom she was dealing with. "Don't undervalue long-term relationships, Byron. Especially among female primates. Besides, the girls consider me a surrogate mother, and you know Old Harry has been something of a surrogate father to me since I was a child."

"I know your bond with them is nothing short of remarkable. But there are studies—"

"Byron. Please. You want to recite studies to me when the science community is, even as we speak, allowing the transfer of ape organs into human beings?"

Grimacing, he rubbed the back of his neck. "Okay, message received."

Ready as always to forgive him, because she knew he spoke more from the heart than anything, she drew him out of the room. "Come see the mess next door. I had to let Old Harry have his own paint and brush. The first thing he did was attack the windows."

The change of topic worked for the most part. Then when they went outside to join the animals—who were arguing for first rights on the new tire swing Byron had just attached to a tree limb—their gleeful mood, along with the blissful weather, helped them recapture their usual companionable mood.

But never far out of the line of her vision was "Dunndrogo's" tree, and secretly it had an inevitable affect, weighing her heart and testing her smile.

She should have known Byron would notice. What she didn't expect was that he would add to her worries.

"I'm sorry for upsetting you before," he murmured, as she watched Daisy and Ditto share a ride on the tire.

"No, you were right to remind me." She had to allow him that as a proven friend.

"But it conjured old worries about Isaac, didn't it?"

Actually, because her mind was burdened with thoughts of Dunndrogo, she'd been managing not to think much of him at all. Now that Byron brought him up, however, she immediately grew uneasy. Her friend knew better than to stir up old nightmares, without good reason.

"Has something happened?" she asked, careful to keep her voice low, since she never knew what Old Harry could pick up. She eyed the orangutan, who was getting tired of pushing the chimps and tried to claim his own turn.

"Probably nothing. I should be kicked for even bringing it up."

"I promise to kick you, if you're sounding a false alarm. Now tell me." Silently, Paloma wondered how, if it was bad news, she would cope with an already full plate of concerns.

He pressed his hand against the tree trunk and tested the bark texture with the pads of his fingers. His movements were more like caresses, and Paloma had a strong hunch that *she* was what he wanted to be touching.

"We received a strange phone call this week at the center."

Because there would be no reason for him to mention such a thing, unless he felt it might have something to do with her, tiny alarms sounded throughout her body. Nevertheless, Paloma replied as calmly as she could. "How strange?"

"Someone called inquiring about my article on chimps and sign language in *Vision Science.*"

Don't panic, Paloma commanded herself. "It was a strong paper, Byron."

"Thanks to your considerable input. But as you well know, that's the same piece that led Tredway to the farm. You want to call that a coincidence?"

She remembered. "It still doesn't mean that it's automatically *him*. You're forgetting I warned him what would happen if he ever tried to find us again."

"No, I haven't. But what if he didn't take you seriously?"

"Who took the call? Did they say the person asked for any details? Addresses? Phone numbers?"

"Of course not. Tredway's not so careless that he'd give himself away twice in a row. But the point is he knows that I'm working in Portland."

"And you feel the fact of his having property in Maine that I know about is too much of a coincidence?"

"If you were looking for someone, would you leave the stone unturned?"

"I don't know. I never imagined I had enough of a conniving mind to escape him in the first place."

Byron took hold of her shoulders. "You said yourself, the animal rights people are making it more difficult for research labs to find test subjects. Maybe Old Harry isn't as valuable to him as he once was, but the girls . . ."

Paloma felt the blood drain from her face.

"I shouldn't have brought it up," Byron muttered, quickly offering a hug. "Maybe it's nothing. But... just in case, be careful, all right?"

"You know I will," she replied, wondering if she and her family would ever get to live in peace.

She decided she would not be a prisoner to anyone's threats.

A few days after Byron's warning, and still brooding over Dunndrogo, Paloma decided she'd had her fill of hiding behind the compound's walls and licking her wounds. Granted, she remained torn and confused over what to do about both matters, but then one day her decision about those proved of secondary importance. It happened Wednesday afternoon, the moment Ditto interrupted her lessons, to ask if they could go float flower petals.

Ditto long water dot, was her actual request. The chimp helpfully pushed word cards away to pinch three fingers together and tap them against her palm to sign her intent.

Not quite sure that meant she wanted to play with a bucket of water and the few wildflowers scattered in the compound, Paloma asked her to repeat the request.

Ditto long water dot now. Hair happy Ditto dot water.

"You sweetheart," Paloma whispered, as it struck her what the chimp meant; and, considering that it was a genuinely *reasoned* request rather than a memorized one, she couldn't be more thrilled. "Yes, Hair very happy there," she said and signed.

This was exactly the breakthrough Byron had been waiting for. To her it was a fine example of disproving the theory that primates learned through analogy, rather than human-style reasoning. For that Ditto deserved to be rewarded.

But she couldn't forget that Dunndrogo had warned her about future venturings into the woods.

She debated over the matter for all of a minute. It took her only that long to decide that granting the wish would do wonders for Ditto's fragile self-esteem, and that was worth a little risk.

With a glance at watchful Daisy, who was only pretending to give her word cards any serious attention, she leaned over to look under the table at the senior member of their group. Old Harry lay on the floor with his feet up on a chair.

What say Old Harry? He hear?

Hear maybe good.

Too sore feet go?

That had been his excuse for avoiding his lessons today. Instead, the lazy rascal had been busy kissing the photos of bikini-clad models in one of the magazines Byron had supplied. But upon learning the excuse might get him left behind, he scampered out from under the table, collected his parasol, and hurried to the door.

Walk slow. Old Jungle Man me.

Outnumbered and outcharmed, Paloma left the cleaning up for later, and followed the group already racing into the yard.

They would be safe, she told herself as she checked the position of the sun. Barely past midday. She knew it was the least likely hour of the day to run into Dunndrogo. Besides, she thought, touching the row of scabs on her palm, she hadn't so much as felt him since that last confrontation.

At least, she continued as they exited the gates, this would give her one more small chance to try to find out what happened to that missing goat. Of course, for all she knew, the wanderlusting pet was long home by now. The next time she went to town, she needed to stop by Westman's store and ask.

A shriek of excitement from Daisy brought her attention back to the immediate, and she hurried to catch up with her exuberant group. But when she discovered what had Daisy so thrilled, she grimaced in dismay.

Her youngest explorer had located a cocoon of caterpillars—the primate's answer to sushi. Since they were already insisting on the treat, and the tree looked relatively safe, she couldn't forbid them.

"Go ahead, but I refuse to watch," she told them, before turning her back on the scene.

She found nothing about dealing with and caring for animals unacceptable, but she much preferred when they craved leaves, seeds, or even soil from a cliff face, which they occasionally needed for its mineral nutrients. When their tastebuds led them to the humanly unpalatable, though, she tried to be a good sport about it.

She should have known that in their euphoria, the chimps wouldn't be able to resist teasing her a bit, especially when Old Harry called from beside her and begged his own treat. But the shadows farther in the woods had drawn her attention. Their size and shape soon had her thoughts wandering, so when the first fuzzy worm landed on her braid, she barely noticed and idly brushed it away. Seconds later, however, a whole handful landed on her white T-shirt and immediately began spreading like a dark stain.

She couldn't stop the screech. Thoroughly shaken, she shook, flicked and plucked them off, all the while backing out of range in case they wanted to present her with more gifts.

The three apes filled the woods with their gleeful cries.

"No!" she cried in a loud whisper. Frantically, she signed for them to stop. They couldn't begin to know how far their voices could carry, or how much she wanted to keep this excursion as low-key as possible. Maybe she didn't intend to remain imprisoned in their compound, but she didn't want to upset Dunndrogo, either. "Come on down here. That's enough now."

Her nerves were tested again minutes later, when Ditto decided she didn't want to stop at their usual spot by the water. Instead, the young chimp entreated a farther excursion upstream. But that was forbidden territory. Dunndrogo's territory.

Paloma tried to redirect her interest in the opposite direction.

Ditto countered with the idea that upstream was where she remembered the best flowers grew.

Feeling manipulated into a corner, and less cheerful about this adventure than before, Paloma relented. "Okay, we go. But all stay close," she told them, trying to look stern.

A half hour later, she allowed herself to relax. Their excursion had just started out badly, that's all. She'd worried over nothing. The area they sat in had never felt so peaceful to her, and the promise of June's wildflowers had yielded July's bounty, including Daisy's namesake.

The girls plucked blossom after blossom, tucking many in each other's hair, then hers and Old Harry's. They enjoyed eating their share, too. After a while, the game changed to pulling petals off the blossoms and tossing them on the water like dozens and dozens of tiny boats—or "dots" as Ditto had christened them.

Paloma stayed next to Old Harry, leaning back against a tree and gazing up at the sky that occasionally peeked through the softly swaying branches. How perfect this moment would be if Dunndrogo could share it with them. What a sweet respite they could have shared, and how sad that he wouldn't even give her a chance.

Did she doze off as a result of the sun and the quiet? When next she opened her eyes, it seemed as though only seconds had passed. At first. Then she realized that Old Harry lay snoring beside her, and Daisy and Ditto were nowhere to be seen.

She called them softly, hoping not to rouse the orangutan. When they didn't answer, she began searching the area. There were still berries on the bushes, and although most were overripe at this point, maybe they'd worked their way around the patch in an attempt to satisfy their endless appetites.

With a glance back at Old Harry, she decided it would be best to let him sleep while she checked around a bit farther. He didn't like doing duty as a bloodhound, and he also could be grumpy if awakened prematurely from a nap. Surely, the girls were close enough that she would be back in a minute.

Sometime later, she found herself coming out of the woods and looking up at the mountains that rose gray and unwelcoming, despite the beautiful summer day. Did her friends decide they needed some mineral and come this way to lick on the stone?

She didn't see a trace of them. But just as she raised her hands to her mouth to risk a call, she spotted a flash of brownish gray to her left.

Too light a color for the chimps, and too large—that much she knew instinctively. Had it been a deer? No, she thought, raising her gaze upward. She didn't think a deer would climb up that high. But a goat might. Douglas Westman hadn't described his pet's color. Had she at least solved that mystery?

The figure had disappeared around a wall of granite. Paloma had to investigate. What if it had followed the girls out of curiosity? The chimps were used to birds, squirrels and rabbits, but a goat would be something entirely foreign, even frightening to them.

She circled the base of the mountain for a bit, until she found the closest thing to a path upward. It looked promising because of the spotty vegetation. The growth would be enough to lure the chimps.

Then she reached the spot where she'd seen the figure and her hopefulness turned to tension. There was a cave behind that wall. She didn't want to think about Daisy and Ditto being in there. They couldn't bear close, dark places any better than she could. But she had to go up and take a look.

Despite a fairly steep climb, she managed it without becoming too winded. At the top, she gazed warily into the entranceway, wishing now that she'd brought along her hiking stick. And a flashlight.

Should she call out and make her presence known? Perhaps that wasn't the best idea.

Moistening her lips, she inched forward. Keeping close to the inner wall, she got to the mouth of the cave, then peered inside.

She saw a flickering light.

She also smelled something cooking.

Dunndrogo?

Just the thought of him sent her pulse racing. She wanted so to see him again, but she wished she knew how he was going to react to her discovering where he stayed.

Only slightly more confident than before, she entered the cave. The path remained narrow and almost immediately began sloping downward into a large cavern. Spread before her was the most amazing scene.

Oh, yes, this was indeed a home. There were oil lanterns, tables and chairs. Even a carpet of sorts, she thought, eyeing the threadbare thing spread beneath one of the sturdier chairs.

Books lined rock ledges and benchlike tables, and were stacked anywhere else that could be used as a bookcase or shelf. A few dishes were neatly stored on another paint-worn cabinet. The sole pot, a black-iron kettle, hung over a fire near the entrance to what looked to be another cave. That explained how the place remained free of smoke, she thought, seeing a faint trail seep up and through the opening.

The whole thing looked like a scene out of another time, and yet . . . She could easily picture Dunndrogo here. Somehow. She couldn't explain why if she'd tried.

The old brocade bedspread caught her eye next. Strung on a rope and braced by nicked, sanded saplings, she saw that it separated a coarse wooden cot from the rest of the area. On the opposite side of the cave she noticed a mat of hay and a blanket.

Two beds? she wondered, confused. Had she assumed—

A crash followed by a cry startled her. Paloma glanced back at the other opening in the cave in time to see an old woman staring up at her in horror. The crash had come from the metal bucket of water she'd dropped. Fortunately, the sloping stone forced the water to seep back out the cave and not toward her fire. But that was the only good news. The woman herself appeared anything but the sort to dismiss such a thing.

"Who do you think you are coming in here?"

"Excuse me," Paloma said, not quite certain whether she should run, or descend the rest of the way and try to reassure the woman. "I thought—"

"Get out!"

"But I—"

"This is private property." Wild-eyed, the woman glanced around and snatched up the first large object her gaze fell upon—an ax by a pile of fire kindling.

"Wait a minute." Paloma raised her hands and backed up a step. "This is all a misunderstanding. I can explain."

"I'm not interested in lies. I know what you're after and it's not going to work. Do you think I went through all this so that someone like you could come along? No, not you or anyone else."

"Mother!"

CHAPTER TEN

Paloma had begun turning the instant the huge shadow fell over her and blocked out the daylight. His thunderous warning proved equally momentous.

"Dunndrogo." Torn between awe and relief, she could only lock her shaking knees and stare.

Would he protect her, or shove her over the edge of the path and down into the cave? She couldn't read his expression well, and didn't know if the fury in his voice was a result of her intrusion or—

His *mother*?

Realizing what he'd said, she spun around again and stared at the woman who also stood frozen in place at the base of the path. This was Dunndrogo's mother? With her wild mane of steel-gray hair, and a face that, even from this distance, looked like a map painted on ancient parchment, the woman reminded Paloma of the crones in the fairy tales she read the chimps. Immediately contrite, Paloma reminded herself of what this woman had been through. And living here of all places...

Like her son, the woman wore skins, but hers covered her from neck to wrist, to ankle, so loosely that Paloma couldn't tell anything about her physical condition; however, there was nothing cloaking the determination and threat in her eyes. That made Paloma wonder if the woman might not have been perfectly capable of carrying out her threat, no matter what her indeterminable age proved to be.

"I don't understand," she murmured, hurt as she dealt with the fact that Dunndrogo had lied to her. "You told me she was dead."

"I told you that I wouldn't talk about her," he said, his normally beautiful baritone flat. "I had an obligation to protect her existence."

That made sense—if they were strangers meeting for the first time. But they weren't strangers. They were two people who, for weeks now, had been connected by something unique and special.

"I had to, Paloma," he added more gruffly in her ear. Then he called out, "Put the ax down, Mother."

It felt so good to feel him permeating her consciousness and reading her thoughts again, that Paloma had to clasp her hands together to keep from turning and embracing him. Only after his mother— although with seeming reluctance—put down her weapon, did she let herself face Dunndrogo again.

"What are you doing here?" he asked, sounding more weary than angry.

"The chimps got away from me. I'd been searching for them, and when I saw something move up here, I thought maybe it was following them. Actually, I thought it was a goat that I've been keeping an eye out for, as well."

"I haven't seen any such creature, but your animals are back with the other."

"You mean with Old Harry?"

"Yes. I...encouraged them when I realized they were wandering too far from you."

Her heart seemed to fill up. So he had been nearby. She should have known he would be. He *was* good, and kind, and generous.

He shook his head. "Don't assume too much. Nothing has changed."

"I've missed you."

She didn't realize she was going to admit that until she heard the words herself. From the sound of his sharply indrawn breath, it was clear he was startled, as well. She thought for an instant that he might touch her, but when he did move, it was to gesture for her to continue down the path.

"Come. My mother won't harm you. She only threatened out of fear."

"All right. But I do have to get back to the others soon," Paloma told him.

"I understand. It's time, however, that she met someone like you. She's been without her own kind for too long."

Paloma wasn't so sure about that. She didn't think she was suited for being a friend. Relationships with people even on a short-term basis were difficult for her. It was Dunndrogo's quiet acceptance and secret warmth she'd yielded and responded to. Like now for example, she noted that although he stayed a circumspect distance behind her, she felt as though she walked in his embrace. It made it impossible for her not to glance back at him several times.

At the base of the path, she stopped and met the unwelcoming stare of the woman who, having given birth to Dunndrogo and survived, had to be considered remarkable under any standards. That reminder

compelled Paloma to remain compassionate despite
the taller woman's unyielding demeanor.

"I'm sorry I frightened you," she began politely.

"If that's true, then go away. Leave us alone and
never come back."

She cringed inwardly, painfully conscious of the
anger leveled at her. "That's not possible, Mrs.—"
Paloma could have groaned. Somehow she knew she'd
made a terrible mistake in assuming Dunndrogo's
mother was, or at least had been, married.

"The name's Maeve. *Miss* Maeve Cooper."

There was no missing the resentment that admission carried. And what was the right way to respond
to it? A part of her wanted to embrace the woman,
because she had more of an idea than most what
Maeve had gone through. Another part wanted to retreat and curl into a corner to soothe herself because
of the anger and resentment she felt flung at her.

Paloma wet her lips and tried to remain understanding and open. "I truly feel privileged to meet
you, Miss—May I call you Maeve?"

She received no reply. Feeling terribly out of her
depth with this complicated woman, she offered, "I'm
Paloma. I assume Dunndrogo has told you about me.
Paloma St. John?"

Blue-gray eyes went wide and then narrowed spec-
ulatively. "Say that last name again."

"St. John," she said, slowly and somewhat confused. She realized she hadn't ever told Dunndrogo,
but why did it seem to mean so much to his mother?
They'd never met before, she was certain.

Nevertheless, the woman grew increasingly agitated, which made Paloma want to do an about-face

and run. When she thrust her finger at her, Paloma knew a real fear.

"You're one of them."

"One of whom?" she asked, certain she didn't want an answer.

"Those *monsters*—St. John and Tredway!"

It suddenly felt as though the walls were squeezing in on her. Paloma battled against a tremendous pressure in her head and in her chest. She couldn't breathe, and she couldn't think. All she could manage was to whisper, "You knew my father?"

Behind her, Dunndrogo also grew tense. "What are you talking about, Mother?"

Maeve acted as though she hadn't heard him. "They were partners, weren't they?"

"How do you know that?" she whispered, certain this new nightmare was going to prove the worst yet. Her world was shifting so far off its axis, she couldn't begin to deal with Dunndrogo's confusion and unease.

"*This* is the girl who moved into the house?" Maeve demanded of her son, ignoring Paloma for the moment. "This is the one you've been defending to me and brooding over? This child of a devil?"

"Stop it!" Paloma cried. "Who are you to say such things?"

"I was their secretary!" Maeve spat back.

Paloma shook her head. "No. No, you weren't. I never met you."

"That's true. We never met. But I was at the church when your father married Marietta," Maeve said, seeming to enjoy the shock that brought. "Your mother would turn every head wherever she went, but she was a frail thing. Apparently, it took several years for her to conceive you, unless you're not her only child?''

"I am," Paloma whispered, helpless not to. The woman's commanding gaze could be every bit as compelling as her son's. "It's my understanding she'd had two previous pregnancies, but miscarried both times. The doctors made her wait before trying again. My father admitted once that even so she never quite recovered from the strain of carrying and delivering me. She died shortly after I was born. W-why do you call my father a monster?'' she demanded with as much quiet dignity as she could muster. "He wasn't involved with any of the experiments my uncle—Dr. Tredway was,'' she said, correcting herself. "He was a research scientist, yes, but it was cancer research, all endorsed through the university.''

"I heard that. You called him *Uncle!*"

The lashing words had Paloma stepping back and coming up hard against Dunndrogo's chest. He steadied her by grasping her upper arms, but she could take no pleasure in his touch because a terrible idea was beginning to form in her mind. Neither was Dunndrogo's touch close to being gentle.

"Isaac Tredway is your uncle, Paloma?''

His hold made it impossible to turn around, and dealing with Maeve's accusing glare was equally difficult. "No! I mean, not really. He's...my father suffered a massive heart attack and died when I was eleven,'' she began, aware she was speaking too quickly, but unable to slow down. She had the impression that if she did, she would be found guilty before she could finish explaining. "It was in his will that

Dr. Tredway become my guardian, and deciding it was easier to care for me if he worked at his home, he moved all his research into his private lab in the basement."

"Oh, yes," Maeve sneered, "his private lab. I discovered what he was one day when it was too late. He'd never permitted me down there and I respected his wishes. He was an esteemed scientist, after all, and I was just a secretary. He was a genius, at hiding his true nature, I'll say that. I'd become pregnant, you see, and had nowhere to turn. When your uncle found out I thought he'd fire me. But he was sympathetic. So supportive. My boyfriend wanted no part of such premature responsibility. Your uncle was the comforting one. 'Don't worry about anything, Maeve,' he'd said. 'I'll take care of you, Maeve.' "

She'd been in love once. Admittedly, Paloma couldn't picture the woman young and hopeful. But the remnants of dreams lost were in her haunted, ancient eyes, and so were memories of how something had gone very, very wrong. "What happened?"

"You know," Maeve said at last. "He used me. He'd given me his serum without my knowledge. He'd put it in tea and dose me with it when I was upset. A harmless herbal sedative, he'd say. Well, I was a perfect subject, wasn't I? Pregnant. Single. Unwanted. Who would miss me?"

"Oh, God." Paloma bowed her head, unable to bear accepting that the nightmare had begun as far back as then.

"Why didn't you tell me about Tredway?" Dunndrogo demanded.

Paloma winced at his harsher grip. "You're hurting me."

He eased his grip somewhat, but demanded, "Mother, answer me! Why didn't you tell me who owned that property down below?"

"What difference did it make? Would it have changed anything? I chose to come up here because I knew Tredway and his sister didn't get along. Maybe I came to believe that given time you would have the opportunity to revenge both of us. In the meantime Tredway and his sister's discord provided us with something more important. Safety."

"You're wrong. It didn't," Dunndrogo said heavily.

His mother began to shake her head, then she went very still. "When? No! The child in the woods that summer. But you never said anything about Isaac Tredway coming to the house!"

"I didn't know who he was!" he cried.

Undaunted, his mother flung back, "For good reason, if you remember. I'd begun to tell you our story, and midway through, you decided you didn't want to hear any more!"

"How could I?" he rasped. "I already carried the guilt of knowing that because of me, your life was ruined."

Paloma knew she was miles behind in comprehending all this, but she was putting together enough to be feeling dizzy and nauseated. Then she suffered Maeve's pointing finger again. What now? she wondered with dread.

"If you had listened, you wouldn't have become so obsessed with *her*," Maeve ground out. "Not once but *twice* you fell under her spell. Oh—why didn't I see it? Why did I simply think you'd come across a lost child from the village?''

''Because I was as stingy with details as I was reluctant to listen to your warnings.''

Paloma didn't know whether his admission or his realization of who she was had a greater effect on him, but he slowly released her and leaned back against cool stone, as though needing its support. She used the opportunity to face him, her heart pounding in her throat.

''You saw me the time we visited the estate?''

She waited for him to say something to her. Anything. He merely stared off into space.

Dunndrogo.

He shut his eyes, and blocked her from his mind, as well.

Feeling as though she was losing her mind, Paloma spun around to Maeve again. ''I swear to you, this is the first time I'm hearing any of this. My father was a good man. I was twelve before I realized what Isaac Tredway was doing behind those locked doors. I *never* knew about you.''

Whether Maeve believed her or not was difficult to tell. The woman simply watched her with impassive eyes.

''Please,'' Paloma forced herself to continue, ''tell me the rest. How did Isaac react when he discovered that you knew about him? What happened?''

''He took me into his office, ostensibly to explain that what I had seen had a legitimate explanation. He was very calm, very convincing, very considerate. I almost began to believe him all over again . . . until he tried to serve me a cup of tea. I was shaken, so I accepted it at first, after all, he and your father were renowned throughout the science community. Then I saw something flicker in his eye and I knew it wasn't just tea. If I hadn't flung that steaming tea in his face, if I hadn't run—'"''

"No." Paloma shook her head, knowing she'd reached her emotional and physical limits. "No more." She took a step back, and then another. "I'm sorry, I thought I could, but I can't—"

Maeve's story brought back too many memories of her own, too many living nightmares she still had to deal with every day. She knew if she didn't get out into the fresh air and sunshine, she would be violently ill.

How she made it, she didn't know. She was vaguely aware of Dunndrogo calling her name, but her need to escape was stronger.

The sun blinded as she rushed from the cave. First stumbling, then falling, she slid several yards on her hands and knees before she managed to regain control. Pain scorched her palms and her knees throbbed, but it was nothing compared to the agony she felt inside.

Maeve Cooper had worked for Isaac. He'd been responsible for Dunndrogo. He'd already proved he was capable of doing what he'd threatened to do to her. His sins went beyond the tragedies and horrors she'd witnessed. They went beyond her ability to cope any longer. She wanted to die. She thought she might be losing her mind.

"I told you," Maeve muttered wearily, "I told you she would bring trouble."

Dunndrogo remained midway up the path, torn between going after Paloma, and his obligation to the woman who had sacrificed everything for him. "It's too late for accusations or regrets."

"We both should have guessed, I suppose. Me most of all. There were too many coincidences. And that child..." Maeve shook her head. "I should have realized you were describing the mirror image of Marietta. Once you met her, the image of that sweet, almost ethereal face never left you."

"Yes," Dunndrogo whispered.

His mother shot him a sharp look. "It changes nothing. She can't be allowed to destroy us now."

Dunndrogo couldn't believe what she was implying. "She isn't related to Tredway, Mother. She had no control over who became her guardian."

"She's a St. John. One's as bad as the other in my book because Richard St. John had to have known about what was going on. Known and approved. And don't forget, the girl lived under Tredway's roof for years, so she knew more than she's letting on."

"Yes, she told me something about that," he murmured, remembering. "But she said, he treated her badly. I don't think there was anything she could do."

"Maybe she didn't try hard enough."

"She was a *child*, Mother. And I've seen her with her animals," Dunndrogo added, although he spoke mostly to himself.

"What animals?"

His mother's incredulous, suspicious gaze spawned a new surge of guilt within him. "When she escaped from Tredway, she rescued some of his test subjects, too."

"Rescued, hmph. So she says."

"They seem to adore her," Dunndrogo said, growing more annoyed that his mother felt compelled to prove Paloma guilty by association.

"You make all the excuses for her that you want. I say she's dangerous to us and should be dealt with. You think about it and you'll see I'm right. *If* she hasn't turned your head too much already."

Dunndrogo couldn't continue listening. He understood his mother's obsession with the past, and sympathized with her growing feeblemindedness. Considering the limitations living here inflicted on her, it was a miracle she hadn't gone stark raving mad years ago. But right now he needed to be alone and resolve some things in his own mind. "Will you be all right?"

"Of course I will. I've always been all right. I always *will* be. No little doe-eyed scrap of a thing like her is going to get to me. Just make sure she doesn't destroy you, my boy. There's no future in dreaming about what you can't have."

Dunndrogo spun away and hurried up the slope. He was afraid that if he didn't get away, he might say something he would later regret.

Once outside, the glare and heat of the sun felt more debilitating than reassuring, and he quickly descended the mountain to take refuge in the dense shady woods. He quickly picked up Paloma's scent, and he drew it deep into his lungs, even as mentally he felt her anguish. It merged with his own and became a pain that made every breath a struggle.

It took him only a short while to catch up with her. She'd rejoined her animals and had begun to lead them back to the compound, but they were asking too many questions about her tears. So she summoned some forced cheer and encouraged them to go ahead of her and play a bit. The one she called Old Harry lingered and looked doubtful, but she assured him that everything would be all right.

Finally alone, she crumbled to the ground and began weeping uncontrollably. He'd never heard such sobbing, couldn't bear it.

Stepping from the bushes, he mouthed her name and soundlessly knelt beside her. What should he say? he wondered, reaching out to touch her hair. When she gasped and scrambled away from him, it was as though she'd stuck a knife in his heart.

"You're wrong," he murmured gruffly. "I didn't come to hurt you."

She looked bewildered for a moment. Then, suddenly, she reached for him, wrapped her arms around him and wept even harder than before.

No one had ever touched him with such relief and need, or sought solace in his arms before. So hungry was he for the precious contact, so convinced had he been that such pleasure and luxury were unattainable for one like him that he couldn't resist clenching his arms tight and drawing her even closer.

Sweet, sweet agony, he thought, absorbing the stunning sensations that seared him as devastatingly as her grief did. If he could die at this moment, he would do so gladly.

Time stopped for them. The shadows cloaked them more gently. The stream even played them a soothing melody.

Dunndrogo felt his heart pound so violently that he wondered if it could bruise her. In comparison, hers seemed more like butterfly wings as delicate as the small breasts crushed against his rock-hard abdomen.

"I'm sorry," she sobbed. "I'm s-so sorry."

"You mustn't do this to yourself," he replied, once again allowing himself the quiet joy of stroking her hair. "I admit your news and my mother's were disconcerting at first, but I know you're innocent of any blame."

"So was my f-father, Dunndrogo. He was a good, decent man. He never did any of the things Isaac did. He would never have condoned them if—if he kn-knew."

"Ssh...I believe you. I do." Dunndrogo shut his eyes and sought the right words of reassurance. "My mother has had a difficult life, Paloma. It's becoming increasingly hard for her to see things clearly."

"She's been through so much. You both have. I'm so ashamed of having known the man who did this to you."

"You've had your own trials."

"They seem nothing compared to yours."

He rested his cheek on the top of her head. "That's your generosity speaking, but don't forget that I feel what you feel. Your thoughts are mine. In the darkest hours of the night, our dreams join and become as one."

That seemed to reach her. Her sobs calmed to ragged, shallow breaths; however, she continued to hold him tight.

"That's true, isn't it?" she whispered, shifting to gaze up at him. "I'd begun to wonder if I wasn't losing my mind."

"It's a strange phenomenon," Dunndrogo agreed.

She eased herself farther back to search his eyes. "How can this be?"

"I don't know." Ever so carefully because he knew too well the strength of his touch and the sharpness of his claws, he wiped away the tears still slipping from beneath her long lashes. "I only know it is."

Paloma's dark eyes softened, making it extremely difficult for Dunndrogo to think, let alone breathe. She was so beautiful to him, and the miracle that she could look at his hideous form and not recoil in revulsion left him astonished and deeply humbled. When she tilted her head to rest her cheek in his palm, a helpless groan of yearning slipped free from the huge lump blocking his throat.

"My sweet, sweet girl," he whispered, and once again succumbed to the need to have her close to his heart.

"Now I know what my father felt with my mother." Paloma stroked her cheek against his chest. "He met her when she was a student where he taught. She was the daughter of a Spanish diplomat and her father disowned her when she eloped with my father. He didn't approve of their age differences, and, too, he'd wanted her to marry someone of her own nationality."

"She must have loved your father very much," Dunndrogo said, knowing he would consider himself blessed to possess even a portion of such a love.

"Yes. They were extremely happy during the few years they had together. I meant what I said, Dunndrogo. I *know* he had no idea about what Isaac was doing."

He wanted to believe her, in fact he did. But he also knew it left many questions unanswered. "I have to trust he wouldn't have left you in Tredway's care if he'd known the truth about his partner," he offered as reassurance.

It must have been enough, considering her soft sigh of relief. "Thank you," she whispered.

"But it means that Tredway is even more of a monster than I'd imagined. While he never got to benefit from what he'd done to my mother, he had you at his mercy for years."

Paloma sat up. "You mean he never found out about you?"

Dunndrogo shook his head. "My mother's escape was successful and she quickly left New Jersey entirely."

"She didn't go to a hospital for help?"

"What help? She was already too far along for an abortion. Besides, would you trust the medical community after the employer—who just happened to be rumored for a Nobel prize—had betrayed you?"

"I suppose not," Paloma admitted. "And so she ended up here, just like me." Suddenly, she frowned. "Maybe our idea wasn't as good as we've been thinking."

"Don't upset yourself again," he replied, rocking her gently. "It's been serving us well enough, hasn't it? Tredway's only come up here once, remember?" He waited for her reaction and was rewarded with a sweet look of incredulity.

"I can't believe you were here back then, that you saw me. It was only weeks after my father died and I was so unhappy. Isaac said he'd been putting off a trip up here and he decided it might do me good to have a ride in the country." She looked around and drew in a deep breath as though comparing the fragrances of then and now. "I've never forgotten that weekend. It was the happiest of my life."

"And mine."

"Dunndrogo—"

She reached up tentatively to touch him. That's when he saw her hands.

"What have you done to yourself?" he groaned, cupping one within both of his.

"I fell when I ran from the cave. It doesn't really hurt anymore."

He took his time to assure himself that her scratches were superficial and that she wasn't in any danger of an infection. Such small hands, he thought again, and such a great weight they carried.

"The first time I saw you," he began at last, "Tredway and his sister had gone inside the house, and you wandered around the compound and out the gates. In her excitement Irene Sims had forgotten to lock her gates. She always locked her gates because of the stories the villagers told her about me. You wore a blue ribbon in your hair," he said more softly, "and a white dress."

Paloma sucked in a sharp breath. "It was the last dress my father bought me."

"You looked like a wildflower. I couldn't stop watching."

"Where were you?"

"Up in a tree. I stayed there until Tredway called you back and the two of you drove away. I wish I'd known who he was then," he added darkly.

"Oh, Dunndrogo," Paloma cried, moving into his arms again. "I only wish you would have said something to me."

"I almost did because you looked so sad. I knew that something terrible had happened in your life, and I wanted to tell you that I knew how such grief felt. It was such a short visit. But I never forgot," he concluded gruffly. He cupped the back of her head with his hand, overwhelmed by the tenderness and yearning she stirred in him.

"Neither did I. Isn't that strange? I used to dream about this place—especially when things got bad."

The slight hitch in her voice created a corresponding ache in his chest. Unable to deny himself the luxury, he turned to bury his face in her hair. "Tell me about those bad times."

"You don't need to hear all that. You've had more than your share of nightmares. Besides, that's all past now."

Was it really? he brooded. Was it ever going to be truly in the past? "I want to know," he said with gentle firmness.

She sighed. "The worst was the darkness, when you knew death was near for someone, but you didn't know who would be chosen next, or what misery it would bring first."

"Did he ever—" Dunndrogo could barely make himself ask "—did he ever inject anything into you?"

"No. I believe he was saving me for when he thought he had his serum perfected. That's why it was so important to him to break my will and create someone docile and subservient. He wanted to be able to let me move in freedom around the house, to create a normal environment in order to study how the average person would function in it. That's how I finally escaped. I tricked him into believing he'd won. But what I was really doing was organizing a plan, arranging for access to keys, scraping together what money and supplies I could, and hiding it all so that he wouldn't notice. Then came locating and hoarding enough of a sedative in his lab to put it in his food and make him sleep through the night.''

Dunndrogo made a sound of incredulity. "You were so young to have shown such initiative and persistence."

"I was old enough to understand what my future held, and to be terrified of what would happen to all of us if I failed."

"No," he insisted. "You were very brave." He shook his head. "What on earth was his motive for all this? What was he trying to create?"

"In the beginning, I believe he sincerely shared my father's interest in cancer research, but as he began to have more and more bizarre reactions to his experiments, it had an effect on him. He was fascinated with the mutations, and he began toying with the idea that he could create an entirely new race of man that was resistant to all disease."

"That's insane," Dunndrogo growled. He had to struggle to control the violence that surged in him. "He's worse than a monster."

"Yes. That's why I destroyed everything that I could find on the serum, when we escaped, and kept one copy of his records. The mistake I made was to keep it with me. That's why he was relentless in tracking us down and finally located us at Byron's farm.

After we escaped, I locked it in a safety deposit box where my trust is held, and gave Byron a letter to present to the authorities if Isaac ever attempts to locate us again, or he ever tries to duplicate the serum.''

"Do you think that's stopped him?"

"I don't know," she admitted. "You heard your mother. He doesn't think like normal people do."

"Perhaps you should have gone to the press,'' Dunndrogo suggested quietly. He knew, of course, the price he would have paid if she had. Chances are, she wouldn't be here now.

Paloma shook her head. "I couldn't do it to Old Harry and the chimps. Inevitably, the stories about what we've been subjected to would come out. We'd become freaks all over again. Byron had also warned me that there might be pressures from institutes to do psychological studies on us. I don't think the animals could bear being put in cages again. I know I've certainly been probed and examined enough for one lifetime."

Dunndrogo seethed. Such evil could not be allowed to continue. "Paloma, I make you this promise . . . if I ever have the opportunity, I'll kill him for you."

"Don't say that!" she whispered, aghast. She gazed up at him, her eyes like black diamonds. "Let's not speak of him anymore. I'm so happy at this moment, I don't want him shadowing that."

Dunndrogo couldn't fathom what he'd done to deserve this gift. "I've long dreamed about you looking at me that way."

Her smile was wistful. "Yet you were so harsh when we first arrived."

"I had to be. After the Sims woman died, I'd meant for that house to remain empty."

"Mrs. Sims. Oh, Dunndrogo . . . the people in town say the most terrible things about her death."

"Let them. She died of a heart attack, but I had no part in it."

"I believe you," she said without hesitation.

He'd done nothing to merit such unequivocal acceptance. He had to warn her about trusting him too much.

"There's another reason I was cruel," he added grimly.

CHAPTER ELEVEN

Paloma could sense Dunndrogo's distress over her calmness, and knew he had a valid concern. She had no clear answer for why she felt no fear of him. She only had her heart, and it was guiding its own course.

"Tell me if you must," she said, never more serene. "But it won't make any difference."

"It should. It has to. Paloma," he began urgently. "Hear what I'm saying. The reason I've tried so hard to push you away—no, to scare you away, is I was afraid of what you made me feel. I still am."

"I give you my word that I'll protect the secret of you and your mother's existence with the same care I do Old Harry and the girls."

"You'll never know how much that means to me. But . . . that's not what I meant."

How could she make him understand? "I know what you meant. This is a good thing that's between us, Dunndrogo."

"But there are so many differences between us!"

"The differences don't matter. I believe we were brought together because we have something rare and precious to give each other. If you believe that—"

"I can't let myself believe that!"

She could tell he was fighting inner demons again. As he pushed himself to his feet and began pacing, there was a tethered violence emanating from him, and she knew every cautious movement cost him dearly.

Suddenly he stopped at a low tree branch. His back to her, he gripped the limb with both hands. "I want you."

"I know."

"No, you don't. If you did, you wouldn't be sitting there, you'd be running for dear life!"

Suddenly, the limb cracked under the sheer force of his grip. Uttering an anguished oath, he spun around and faced her. Naked passion burned in his eyes.

"I want you with a man's desire, Paloma. But look at me—I'm trapped in this monster's body! We can never be together and it's killing me," he concluded in a hoarse whisper.

"You're *not* a monster!"

She could feel him fight his own mind, and willed him to stop. Couldn't he see that they'd been destined for this from the beginning?

His expression grew haunted. "You're not listening! I can't have you. Not in *that* way!"

"It doesn't matter," she replied, never feeling more confident than she did at this moment. He, on the other hand, couldn't have looked more upset.

"How can you say that?"

"Because it doesn't."

"It should," he snapped. "You're just too young to realize what you're saying."

"Age has nothing to do with it, and you know it." She wasn't intentionally trying to provoke him, but she was determined to stand firm in her belief.

"Paloma..." He took a step closer with the caution of a man on a ledge. "You deserve a full life with a normal relationship. That man, your friend who comes to visit you and helped you after you escaped from Tredway's, for instance.''

The woods had never been so still. Paloma felt as though the entire world had stopped upon hearing his incredible words. ''You'd push me into someone else's arms?''

''It would be the best thing, the right thing to do.''

''As fond of and grateful as I am to Byron,'' she replied, speaking slowly so as to keep her own temper, ''I don't feel the same things for him that I do for you. It wouldn't be fair to ask him to settle for less.''

Dunndrogo shook his head, his expression resolute. ''I won't let you throw away your life in a sacrifice to me.''

Everything around her turned gray. Numbed by his decisiveness, as much as his words, it took Paloma a moment to realize it wasn't merely her reaction to what he'd said. She glanced up as a sudden gust of wind whipped several pine needles past her. Heavy storm clouds were claiming the summer sky. Since she had neither a television nor a radio, she hadn't known to expect a change in the weather.

''The air this morning had a sweet heaviness to it,'' Dunndrogo said, not surprisingly picking up her thoughts. ''You'll learn to read the signs...if you stay.''

If she stayed? Disconcerted to hear that train of thought, she was about to tell him so when she heard a call from down the trail. Daisy, she guessed, immediately feeling the pull of obligation. Apparently her sensitive housemates also knew the weather was rapidly deteriorating, and she needed to reassure them.

"It's best," Dunndrogo told her, his tone as fatalistic as his expression was grim. "It will be raining soon."

Although she knew he was right, and even rose, she didn't want to leave him. "When will I see you again?"

He bowed his head. "I don't know. I have much to think about. Decisions to make."

"Now you *are* frightening me," she said, discerning more from what he wasn't saying. A horrible thought crept into her mind. "Dunndrogo. Don't leave me."

He averted his face. "Whatever I decide, I want you to know it's because I think it's best. For all of us, Paloma. Be careful, my—"

As he abruptly began walking away, she felt like the ground had opened beneath her feet. She would never see him again. She knew it.

"No!" she cried. "Dunndrogo!"

He retreated into the brush, as though he hadn't heard her. Devastated, Paloma began to follow, but at that moment Daisy and Ditto came rushing from the opposite direction, chattering and anxious.

Down trees fall, they signaled, before tugging and pushing at her, urging her toward the compound.

Knowing they were right to have come for her, she cast a last, longing look northward. *If it comes from the heart, it's not a sacrifice, Dunndrogo. Don't leave me.*

He walked for hours. Even after it began pouring, he stayed in the woods, indifferent to the rain that soaked him, and the wind that sent branches and vines lashing at him. He wanted the power of it, hoping it might surpass the slashing pain on the inside.

It didn't. It couldn't.

Love, he realized sometime during his directionless wandering, hurt every bit as much as the poets and novelists claimed.

He'd discovered his bliss, true. Fate had let him hold Paloma in his arms, stroke her hair, draw her sweet scent deep into his lungs, and had blessed him with her adoring gaze. For a few precious moments, it had let him ignore who and what he was, and he'd been the happiest being on earth.

But reality was tenacious. As tenacious as his hunger.

He couldn't have her, and because he couldn't, he knew he must never let himself near her again. Despite the fact that from this moment forward, each breath he took would be a labor, every step had to be carefully chosen to direct him away from her.

It was well after dark before he could bring himself to return to the cave. As bad as he felt, he knew he was going to feel worse once his mother began voicing her fears and frustrations.

Although the worst of the storm was over as he began climbing the mountain, the path remained slick. The wind also proved troublesome, and would have challenged a smaller body to stay upright. He was making that observation as he sensed, then spotted the prone figure a few yards away from the cave opening.

Paloma?

With dread energizing him, he flew the last few yards, and he crouched over her. Only then did he recognize the leather cape. "Mother!"

She was shivering from exposure, her teeth chattering so violently that she could barely speak. "H-help m-m-me."

"What happened? Are you hurt?"

"M-my ankle. Slipped."

Why had she been out here in the first place? He never left the cave without being certain that she had adequate supplies. Surely she hadn't been coming to look for him?

Despite the rain-drenched cape, and her limp weight, Dunndrogo had no difficulty lifting her. He carefully carried her into the cave and quickly brought her down to her cot.

She moaned as he laid her on it. "S-soaking the b-bed," she managed to protest.

"It doesn't matter," he told her, even as he removed the drenched item. To his dismay, he found her almost as wet beneath it. He swore under his breath. "How long have you been lying out there?"

"W-worried you'd g-gone to her. M-maybe a trap."

If she hadn't already been suffering, Dunndrogo would have given her a good shake for refusing to see Paloma in her true light. "She doesn't deserve that," he said instead. "She's a gentle, good person, Mother. And you were wrong. I wasn't near the compound. Now let me cover you with this blanket and I'll see to your ankle."

He spread the blanket over her, tucking as much as he could beneath her, except for one corner, which he folded back to inspect her lower right leg. Yes, the ankle was swollen and red. But not broken, he decided, gently testing the joint and foot.

His mother moaned again, but not as much as he knew she would have if the injury had been more severe. "You've only sprained it."

That was the good news. Her chills concerned him more. He glanced across the room toward the kettle from which rose a pleasant and familiar aroma. "I'll bring you some soup. It'll warm you soon enough."

"No. N-not hungry."

He ignored her, knowing if he didn't get something warm and nourishing into her soon, her condition would deteriorate. But despite working for the next hour or so, she did get worse.

He'd never felt more inept. In all their years together, he couldn't remember her being this ill. A self-contained, willful woman, she rarely got colds, and when she did, she coped in stubborn silence. This was different. Serious.

Dunndrogo?

He went very still. Held his breath. He hadn't meant for his thoughts to carry so far.

What's wrong? Something is, I can feel it.

She didn't need to be burdened with his troubles. If he'd been in a stronger frame of mind, he would have shut her out. But it felt so good to feel her warmth and caring.

My mother. She injured herself outside and she's running a fever.

Do you need help?

More than she could imagine. More than he dared confess.

I don't know.

I'll come.

No! I won't let you put yourself at risk.

Then bring her here.

He looked at his mother. She would hate the idea, fight him every step of the way—if she'd been lucid. But she was barely conscious, and he had a feeling that if something wasn't done, she would die.

Dunndrogo?

She watched him step from the darkness, a darker shadow, all the larger now for the burden he carried. Paloma had been standing guard at the gate, and quickly opened it to admit them.

"How is she?" she whispered as he slipped through.

"Getting worse, I think."

He wasn't even winded, remarkable considering the distance he'd come bearing his mother's weight, along with the thick blanket he'd bundled her in. Paloma's awe and respect for him grew, as she locked up behind him.

Now that the rain had stopped, the mosquitoes were out in force and a few zeroed in around Maeve's head. Brushing them away, she said, "Come inside. I've got everything prepared. And I moved the animals to another room. But Dunndrogo, if they do decide to come out, try not to be upset if they act . . . intimidated."

"There's no need to caution or apologize. I understand."

His brief tender look sent a warm current through her. Barely feeling the ground beneath her feet, she hurried to open the front door for him.

Not surprisingly, he had to stoop slightly to make it through the doorway, and would have had to shift sideways even if he hadn't been carrying his mother.

That made the caution and care he showed his mother all the more exemplary.

"Put her over here," she said, leading him to her cot. After he set Maeve down, she helped him remove the blanket. "Oh, dear heaven," she whispered, trying not to disturb the barely conscious woman, "her clothes are soaked."

"I know."

"Never mind, I'll take care of it." Belatedly, she realized his reason for not having changed her. "Maybe you'd better, um . . ."

"I'll wait outside."

Heading for a military-surplus locker where she kept her clothing, Paloma faltered. "That's not necessary. You could just turn around."

"Your animals don't need the stress of having me too near. You have enough to deal with as it is. I'll be more comfortable out there anyway."

As doubtful as she was, Paloma couldn't take the time to protest. Maeve's condition was as serious as he'd said, and needed her full and immediate attention.

It took her several minutes to get the woman out of her wet clothes and into the flannel nightgown that would have been hot for July. But Paloma chose it because Maeve was shaking from cold; in fact, it proved hardly enough. After tucking two blankets around her, she then hurried to the stove to add another stick to the fire. Afterward, she put on a kettle for tea.

How had Maeve hurt herself? Where had she been that she'd got so wet? Why did she get a feeling that most, if not all, of the answers had something to do with *her?*

While waiting for the water to boil, she wrapped the swollen ankle with a bandage she took from their first-aid kit, and raised the injured limb with a pillow and a folded wool throw.

During her ministrations, Maeve briefly opened her eyes. "G-get away from me," she mumbled.

She sounded as though her mouth were full of molasses, but there was nothing sweet about her disposition. Paloma had to swallow her fear to attempt a reassuring smile. "Save your strength, Maeve. You'll need it to beat your fever."

"Am I dying?"

"No! Don't even think such a thing."

"I know I am."

"Listen to me." Paloma leaned forward, tucking the blankets higher under the older woman's trembling chin. "You can't die. Your son needs you."

"No. N-not anymore."

"He carried you all the way down here to get you warm and dry. He loves you, Maeve. Now I'm heating some water to make you some herbal tea, so stay covered while I finish."

"You won't g-get away with p-poisoning me."

As startled as she was, Paloma tried not to show it. "Maeve," she said, shaking her head because she truly wanted to reach through to the woman, "I'm not the enemy, and I'm going to do whatever it takes to convince you of that."

"Why?"

"Because I need you, too," she went on, thinking about Dunndrogo, and about how much she and

Maeve could support each other if only they could get past her suspiciousness.

The older woman didn't exactly answer, but she did give her a strange look. Paloma took that as good news and continued her ministrations.

The fever grew worse. To fight it, Paloma had Dunndrogo pump bowl after bowl of cool water, which she used to wipe down Maeve's flushed, perspiring skin. Despite her injury, Maeve proved a handful, again and again kicking off her blankets, and once Paloma actually had to call Dunndrogo to help hold her down. During that episode Daisy opened the back bedroom door and, spotting him, squealed, then slammed it shut. Dunndrogo never reacted outright, but as soon as his mother began quieting, he immediately withdrew back outdoors.

As much as she wanted to follow him, it was another few hours before Paloma could do so. Maeve required attention for some time afterward, and then Paloma had to go to check on the animals.

It had to be early morning when she finally eased outside, closing the door quietly behind her. Although humid and dark, the air was wonderfully cool after the heat inside. She stood absolutely still for several seconds to let the last hours of tension seep from her body.

She finally felt rather than saw Dunndrogo at the far end of the porch, leaning against the house and watching her. Turning, she smiled. "She's sleeping peacefully."

He exhaled with relief and crossed over to her. As he passed a window, the faint light from inside illuminated his pale blue eyes.

"How am I going to thank you?" he asked gruffly.

With each step, she grew more aware of him, more aware of his gaze holding hers, more aware of the admission he'd made earlier today.

"I was glad to help."

"It couldn't have been easy. I saw your reaction to some of the things she said."

Because she didn't want him brooding over his mother's understandable dislike for her, Paloma tried to tease him a bit. "You have a disconcerting habit of peeking in windows."

"I like to watch you."

She couldn't have felt more off balance if she'd slipped on a patch of ice. For someone who was trying desperately to make her turn to someone else, he could be irresistibly seductive.

"She's a strong woman and she loves you very much, Dunndrogo. You can't blame her for trying to protect you."

"I know. Except for the midwife who helped bring me into the world, we've been each other's only company for years. As you can imagine, they haven't all been serene ones."

"Close quarters and total isolation would put a strain on any relationship," she replied, lifting a shoulder to dismiss his concern. "Old Harry and I have had our share of tense moments."

"You're being generous. Your orangutan would test the patience of a lump of clay."

Sometimes, Paloma thought with a smile, she could agree. "Tell me about the midwife who helped your mother. Was she someone from around here?"

"An old gypsy-like woman who lived on the outskirts of the village. She's been gone almost twenty years now. If it wasn't for her strength and skills, both Mother and I would never have survived labor."

"She sounds as though she was a remarkable woman."

"We've been gifted by having a few remarkable people come into our lives."

They stepped off the porch and Paloma looked up at the night sky to try to slow down her jumpy heartbeat. It was useless; the stars were out again, and could be seen between long fingers of pewter and indigo clouds. The vision merely intensified the aura of romance and poignancy surrounding them.

"As relieved as I am that your mother is better, I wish tonight didn't have to end," she murmured, drawing in a deep breath of the purified air.

"I know. I feel the same, but it's time I left. It will be dawn soon, and you need some rest."

They'd reached the front gate, and although Paloma drew out the key and unlocked it, she hesitated in actually releasing the latch. Instead, she rested her forehead against the bars and searched for the words to explain what she felt.

"You don't have to, I feel it," he whispered, the sound heartbreakingly sad.

Relieved, she turned to press her cheek to his chest. "Then stay. At least awhile longer."

"You're exhausted. If you don't lie down soon, you'll get ill yourself."

"I've never felt more awake or stronger in my life, Dunndrogo. Because of you. Because of *you*."

"Just for a moment," he murmured, reaching for her and drawing her against his solid frame. "Then I'll go, and you'll let me. Are you listening, Paloma? You'll let me go."

"Yes."

"Ah, God." He shifted his hold to urge her head against his chest. "Such bliss. Such pain. I can't keep you as I want, but I can't bring myself to let you go, either."

"You don't have to."

"Yes, I do. I won't watch what happened to my mother happen to you. Not twice in one lifetime, I won't let you waste your life on a travesty born from some perverted mind!" With a sound that seemed to be torn from his throat, he put her at arm's distance. "I'm going."

He all but tore the latch from its mooring and rushed out. Paloma caught the swinging gate.

"Dunndrogo! Don't!"

He stopped in midstep. "Lock it."

"What?"

"Lock it."

She couldn't challenge the fierce warning underlying his words and hastily snapped the bolt, as directed. But she was by no means surrendering. "Please."

He backed up a step. Two. Came flush against the gate and exhaled in a rush as though impaled. The metal shuddered and groaned in protest. "Paloma, we have to stop."

"No."

"You don't know what you're saying."

"Dunndrogo, stop locking me out of your life!"

He spun around and gripped the bars. "Stop tempting me!"

Unable to think of anything else to do, she rose on tiptoe and kissed the hair-covered fingers that gripped fiercely at iron. "I'm not afraid. I won't run. You can't push me away."

He reached through the bars. His fingers skimmed her cheek. "If only..."

"If only what?"

Abruptly he spun away, vanishing behind the wall. Paloma skirted to the side, too.

"Dunndrogo? Dunndrogo!"

"If only I was normal."

Tears flooded her eyes. She rocked her forehead against stone. "You're more normal than anyone I've ever met."

"No. But if I was... I would show you."

Paloma felt every nerve ending in her body. "Show me what?"

"How much I cherish you."

Splaying her fingers, she slid her hand to where she imagined, thought, *felt* his chest was. "Tell me instead."

The sound of his strained breath rose over the compound wall and floated down to her. "This isn't an easy thing to talk about."

"You mean you're embarrassed?"

"Aren't you?"

"Yes, until I remind myself that it's not as though we're standing face-to-face. You're on that side of the wall, and I'm on this side."

"Does it make it easier?"

"No. But knowing you care does."

"I care. More than words can express. If I could, I would be holding you now and showing you how much."

She understood what he wasn't saying, and felt a surprising relief and joy to know he was as inexperienced as her. "If you could," she whispered, "what would you do? What would you say?"

"I'd... touch you."

"Where?"

"Your face."

"But you have before."

"Not your lips. Not your throat."

Paloma closed her eyes and let herself imagine that happening. "Do you know how safe, how right I feel when you hold me?"

"Do you know that your skin carries the fragrance of soap and flowers, and just breathing it in makes me ache. It makes me want to taste you... everywhere."

Her imagination roared to life. Like a runaway fire, heat spread through her body, stealing her breath and leaving her panting shallowly.

"You like the thought of my hands and mouth on you? You can picture it happening? Feel it?"

His erotic whispers won shiver after delicious shiver from her. "Yes."

"Then perhaps there is a way for us after all. Take me into your mind, Paloma. Take me where you want me to go. Wherever you want me to go."

It was so seductive an idea, so irresistible and natural, that she did so easily. Behind her closed lids, she pictured them in a pool of indigo light, facing one another. Smiling in confidence and trust.

She wore a gossamer nightgown. He wore his leather and the night.

She reached up to him and he lifted her high off the ground, so high she felt dizzy with delight and threw back her head to laugh breathlessly. The sound turned to a sigh of pleasure, when he pressed his mouth to the deep V of her gown.

More.

He not only complied, he turned his head to the left and brushed an openmouthed kiss to the inside curve of her breast. Then another a few inches over. Then another. With each progressive kiss, he freed her body from the gown, until the filmy material slipped off her shoulder.

Beautiful . . . so beautiful.

Kiss me. Let me feel your mouth there.

Her nipple beaded at just the thought of how it would be, and when his mouth covered her, she trembled from the rush of ecstasy that swept through her body like a tidal wave. His lips suckled, his tongue stroked, and even though the dual sensations won a gasp from her, she cupped the back of his head and drew him closer.

The night air was cool on her moistened flesh when he turned to offer the same caresses to her other breast. Then the silky gown slipped off her right shoulder, his mouth claimed her, and heat spawned anew.

I can feel your heartbeat against my womb.

I can feel yours inside my mouth.

The provocative admissions intensified Paloma's desire, allowing yet a new self-confidence. She twisted and pressed closer, her body restless to learn everything. All-powerful, all-patient, Dunndrogo fulfilled each yearning.

He lifted her higher and the gown slipped farther. His kisses grew more ardent and their bodies became like one long torch whose blinding flame reached toward the heavens.

Burn for me, my lady, my dream. Want me. Need me.

I do. I do.

Touch me.

As he lowered her to his eye level so she could, she shifted the hands that had been on his massive shoulders to his dark, fierce face. She directed her worshipping fingers over each amazing feature, and with each caress his crystalline-blue gaze burned with a deeper passion virtually stealing her breath. When she began following each caress with a soft kiss, his own breathing grew strained, and his muscular body turned rigid, as if he was fighting an unbearable pain.

It is a pain—pain born of wanting you too much.

I want you, too.

Then kiss me. Kiss me as though I were a man.

Dunndrogo, to me you're more than any man.

He sought the truth of those words in the gift of her lips. His own were restless in their hunger, and yet she could feel him fight the wildness that went beyond emotion, deeper than blood, all the way to the mutation of genes that forever cursed him to a life of perpetual torment.

But not here in the safety of our minds.

Her gentle reminder freed him, as she'd intended. Magic claimed the night, and with the tender violence he'd been repressing, he kissed her. And kissed her.

Long draining kisses that made them both tremble and soon had them straining to get closer.

The guttural plea escaping Dunndrogo's throat answered Paloma's unspoken question.

It had to be soon. Now. Quickly, before joy grew into unbearable agony.

She let him lower her to the soft carpet of grass. Her hair was the rest of her mattress. His was their blanket. It caressed like raw silk as he skimmed a trail of kisses up her legs. Then it obliterated the world like a moonless night as he rose above her.

Still his pale, unworldly eyes burned into hers, and his hard, hot flesh probed with irrevocable intent. But it was his tender care that gained him entry.

Paloma's breath caught at his sensitive possession. Instinctively she arched to welcome him deeper. Behind closed lids the red tide of pain yielded quickly to an indigo sea of sensation and pleasure.

She heard him whisper and groan her name. *She* had no voice, no thought, only the unbelievable sensation of being fully, completely possessed.

Then he began to move.

It was all grace and power, and she quickly felt their mutual, irrepressible need to race toward oblivion, to reach that plateau of ecstasy they'd believed was forbidden them.

Then in that breach of consciousness, as the heat and light of satisfaction united them in some psychic universe, Paloma opened her eyes and saw Dunndrogo thrust his hand through the wrought iron gates.

Smiling through her tears, Paloma gave him hers.

CHAPTER TWELVE

"Where's my son?"

Paloma finished pouring from the kettle on the stove before turning to Maeve. It took her that long to mask the multitude of emotions churning within her and to decide how to approach the woman now that the threat of a more serious illness was behind her.

"Good morning," she said, deciding to try a warm smile as a start. "I see you're feeling much better. How's the ankle? Do you think the bandage is too tight?"

"Not really."

She hadn't earned a smile back, but her reply had been civil enough. Pleased, Paloma nodded. "Great. I'm happy to say you're vastly better than you were last night. That fever you had would have fried a weaker person's brain."

"Dunndrogo shouldn't have brought me here," Maeve said, clearly uncomfortable as she glanced around.

It could be far worse, Paloma told herself with an inner sigh. She could be accusing her of poisoning her again. "As I told you last night, Maeve, you were very ill. Dunndrogo was beside himself with worry. And I was glad to be of help. Really."

"I don't remember very much." The woman noticed the nightgown for the first time and a strange look came over her face. Her work-worn fingers skimmed over the lace-trimmed bodice with near reverence. "Oh, my. It's been years since I've worn anything so fine."

Bemused, Paloma finished stirring the tea she'd been preparing for Maeve and carried it to her. "Actually, I worried you'd be insulted, but it's the newest I had and you were so cold. If you really like it, you're welcome to take it when you go ho—back."

Maeve stared as she set the steaming mug on the wood crate the chimps used as a desk, her shrewd gaze softened by confusion. She must have been, Paloma thought, a handsome woman once.

"Thank you," she murmured, frowning more now. "Perhaps you should get Dunndrogo for me. I'm creating an awful lot of work for you."

"Not so much, and I'm enjoying having the company. Besides you can't go anywhere on that ankle for a few days. We've already agreed."

"*We?* That certainly sounds cozy."

The mere mention of Dunndrogo thrust Paloma's thoughts into memories of last night, and she knew she couldn't discuss him without betraying her feelings for him. She was almost grateful that Maeve's feelings toward her kept teetering back and forth between open dislike and grudging appreciation.

"I'm not expecting miracles, Maeve," Paloma said carefully, stepping back to sit at the foot of the bed. "But I do hope we can learn to be civil to each other for Dunndrogo's sake."

She didn't get a response because the animals chose that moment to emerge from their room. Old Harry was the first to appear. He gave their visitor as much room as possible before posting himself on his chair like a discontented monarch viewing his court from his throne.

For her part, Maeve recoiled, pressing back into her pillows at the first sight of him. "You let him run loose? Isn't he dangerous?"

"Only if you make the mistake of threatening him." Paloma went to stroke the orangutan's back reassuringly, before turning to greet the others.

Daisy and Ditto came holding hands. When they were parallel to the cot, they broke into a run and leapt simultaneously at Paloma, almost toppling her onto their bed.

Laughing, she introduced her primate family, and explained as carefully as possible, without the animals picking up too much, what their history at the hands of Isaac Tredway had been. Maeve listened with some indifference at first, and then with deepening distress.

"Stop!" she cried at last, when Paloma was about to describe the fate that had befallen Daisy's and Ditto's mother. "I can't bear to hear any more. It brings back too many nightmares."

"I didn't mean to upset you," Paloma said with sincere regret. She watched Old Harry reach for one of the bananas she'd laid out for him, and signaled him to bring some for the girls. "I only wanted you to understand that we have more in common than you'd realized."

"How could you *bear* it? Being imprisoned like an animal for days, weeks at a time and . . . Oh, it's too terrible."

"Old Harry kept me sane by teaching me how to communicate with him," Paloma told her, accepting the empty peel he decided she could hold. She briefly explained their telepathic connection. "Also, I was fortunate to recognize early on how patience was the real key to freedom," she added. "You see, it was useless to attempt running away until I could both care for the survivors, and support all of us financially. That meant being old enough to get my hands on my trust fund."

Maeve shuddered, then shot her a guilty look. "I think I owe you an apology."

Pleased as well as relieved for this mellowing, Paloma was more than willing to dismiss their previous lack of rapport. "No need. I don't know if I could have survived what you did. You're a remarkable woman, Maeve."

"How odd. My son said the same thing about you."

Once more the memories of last night flooded her mind, and as they did, Paloma's body began tingling anew—especially as she remembered some of Dunn-drogo's dark, passionate thoughts. They had been speechless after what they'd shared; after all, common sense told her that what they'd achieved should have been impossible. Words would have ruined the magic. Instead they'd clung to each other's hand for a long time afterward.

"Dunndrogo's very special," she murmured, feeling her throat tighten as she held back all the things she wanted to say about him.

"Dear Lord. You're in love with him."

Paloma knew the truth was in her eyes, so she simply nodded. Then, abruptly, her attention was drawn elsewhere. A secret smile curved her lips. "He'll be here in a few moments."

Maeve's eyes went wide. "Do you mean you two can do that, as well?"

"Yes." Paloma studied her disconcerted expression. "I hope that doesn't upset you."

"I don't know. It's seems unnerving, but... er, can you read mine?"

"No," Paloma said, almost laughing outright. "Basically, it has to be a mutually agreed thing."

"He never said anything to me."

Maeve reached for her tea, and Paloma knew it was because Maeve needed to reconcile a number of things in her mind. Particularly the idea that after focusing a lifetime of energy on her son, there was now someone else in his life.

Paloma felt only compassion, and she wanted to reassure Maeve that a mother's love was irreplaceable, except that she didn't want her to think she was reading her thoughts, after all.

Then Maeve looked up at her, concern replacing the sadness in her eyes. "Are you aware of all the differences between the two of you, beyond the obvious ones?" she asked hesitantly.

"I think so." Paloma did, however, feel a pang of unease. She was, wasn't she? "I know about his need to... hunt. And I know he's very concerned about physically hurting someone."

"That you must remember most of all. His emotions are as unparalleled as his great physical strength. Never forget he's capable of anything. Not even I can be sure he's always in control of himself."

"I understand," Paloma assured her. But secretly she couldn't help feeling with enough love even that dark part of Dunndrogo's nature could be tamed.

She hurried to the front door, eager to open it to Dunndrogo. Spoken words would have betrayed the depth of emotion between them, and so they relied on their personal method of relaying messages.

I'm so glad to see you.

It's the same for me. You filled my dreams.

And you mine. "Come in," Paloma added, stepping back to let him enter. "Your mother's much, much better."

Unfortunately, in her excitement to see him again, the one thing she forgot was the animals' reaction to him. Ditto whimpered and bolted under Maeve's cot. Daisy sprang across the bed and hugged the startled woman's neck. Old Harry, belying his age, leapt behind his chair and peered out warily.

Ghost not hurt Old Jungle Man.

Initially heartbroken by the commotion, Paloma was greatly relieved by the unique message. She glanced back at Dunndrogo to see if he could pick up on it. *Ghost.* Had that one been plucked from her thoughts or did he create it himself?

If Jungle Man friend of Hair, then friend of Ghost.

Paloma thought her heart might stop. She looked from the striking figure standing nobly, but tentatively in her doorway, to her oldest friend, still hiding behind the worn chair.

"What's going on?" Maeve asked uneasily. Whether she was aware of it or not, she wrapped her arms protectively around Daisy, as she would a child.

For his part, Old Harry crept up onto his chair again. As far as messages went, it wasn't much, but Paloma pressed a hand to her stomach, relieved to have the butterflies there settle.

"We were just going through some introductions," she replied, taking Dunndrogo's arm. "Come see your mother. She's doing much better this morning."

He overpowered the room with his presence, but his aura was full of tenderness as he approached the elderly woman on the cot. It proved a strange moment for Paloma. the son, who was forced to be distant because of something out of his control, and the mother who continually struggled to understand how to deal with her very special son.

From beneath the bed came the sound of a soft whine. Paloma hurried to the foot of the cot and coaxed Ditto to come to her. With the chimp in her arms, she backed up to sit with Old Harry.

"You gave me a scare last night," Dunndrogo said to his mother.

"I know. Paloma and I have been discussing the situation we've found ourselves in. I'm afraid I wasn't ready to put any faith in it, let alone accept it, but," she added, glancing around him to Paloma, "I see that I was wrong. You seem to know what you're doing, and I won't deny you this corner of happiness you've found for yourself."

Dunndrogo knelt beside the bed and took one of her hands within his. "Thank you, Mother. I'd hoped being here in Paloma's home would allow you to see that she's a healing source in many senses of the word."

Maeve drew in a deep breath and patted the hands that held hers. "I see that together you create a chemistry I've never witnessed before. It's rather humbling."

Sensing how moved Dunndrogo was, Paloma offered help by adding cheerfully, "Look at how Daisy's taken to her, Dunndrogo. Help me convince her to spend a few more days here. It will give her ankle time to heal. The chimps would love the company. How are you with bedtime stories, Maeve?"

Seemingly intrigued with the idea, the woman actually tittered as the chimpanzee studiously inspected her long, flowing hair. "Well...there was many a night that Dunndrogo wouldn't go to sleep without first having me read him a story. The ones about knights and dragons and damsels in distress were always your favorites, do you remember, dear?"

Paloma sensed something wrong before Dunndrogo actually replied. She also saw it in the tenseness of his back muscles.

"Yes," he replied, releasing her hand. "I remember."

When he rose, Paloma immediately set Ditto on the bed and went to him.

"What's wrong?"

It was Maeve who spoke the words, but Paloma was already seeking answers her own way.

Dunndrogo didn't answer either of them. He looked as though he might try; however, a moment later he simply headed for the door.

"Dunndrogo?" she whispered. "Please. Talk to me."

"It's nothing. I . . . I need to go."

"But you've only just arrived. I thought you could visit with your mother while I—"

She never got to finish. He jerked open the door and walked out. Once in the yard he broke into a lope, then a dead run. Stopping on the porch, she watched him go over the wall as though it was barely more than a track hurdle.

Dunndrogo?

He didn't answer.

Wait for me. I'll find you. Wait for me.

Dejected and not knowing what to think, Paloma shut the door. When she turned, she found Maeve watching her sadly.

"Now do you see what I mean?"

He ran. He ran as though all the demons of hell were behind him. Only he wasn't that lucky. They nested inside him.

For hours after he left the compound, Dunndrogo sought relief in the woods. They were like a balm on an open wound. A balm that needed refreshing every few hours, every few minutes. To ensure that, he moved from the visual safety of the outside wall, to the cave, to his secret cavern, then back outdoors for more air and space.

Throughout the day he felt Paloma trying to contact him. He wanted to let her in, to lock on, but the inner fear, the wildness that always ate at him refused to let go.

It was near sunset when she finally tracked him down. He stood on a ledge near the cave watching the western horizon, but acutely aware of her every step. Wanting her to hurry. Dreading her arrival. Even as his mind logged the generosity of her thoughts for posterity, he felt himself wishing he'd never met her.

What a mysterious, fierce figure you cut standing there blending in with the long shadows. I'm beginning to realize I could spend the rest of my life trying to learn the different sides of you, and I'd never uncover all there is.

She didn't quite join him on the ledge. She stopped a few yards back and below, seemingly content to sit, recuperate from her climb, and wait for him to decide how he would handle her presence.

"Canada is that way," he said at last. "I almost convinced myself to leave for there today."

It took just as long for her to respond. "Without saying goodbye?"

He could do this, he thought. For her sake, he could. But he wasn't surprised that the very idea left a bitter taste in his mouth. "You're already on your way to winning over my mother," he forced himself to reply. "I can see she would be safer in your care than mine."

"Without saying goodbye," Paloma said, a break in her voice.

The hurt and anguish he heard were more difficult to bear than he'd anticipated. If only she could have found the anger to curse him. "Paloma. I'm trying to do what's best for both of us."

"In other words, you regret last night."

Her voice failed on "regret," and the last few words were a dry rasp. With a sob, she scrambled to her feet, and ran.

Dunndrogo swung around. He wanted to imprint her departing form onto his mind forever. Instead he had to will himself not to go after her.

But he hadn't counted on what she was doing. She sprinted as though on straight, even ground. Sheer insanity. The mountain was too steep, too slippery to be traversed with such recklessness. She wouldn't just fall, didn't she realize that? She would kill herself!

Even as the thought formed in his head, his blood turned cold. The little fool didn't *care* if she fell.

Filled with terror and fury, he took off after her.

With several seconds' head start, and possessing the agility of a gazelle, she automatically built herself an impressive lead. Nevertheless, she was no match for his strength or speed.

He felt every gasping breath she took, felt every painful thud of her heart. And two thirds of the way down, he knew the instant the rubber sole of her sneaker slipped on rock.

Dunndrogo leapt, and reached, testing himself as he'd never challenged his body before. He grabbed her as she began pitching forward, snaking his arm around her waist.

"No!" she screamed.

Even if he'd wanted to stop, it was too late. The momentum of his dive was already propelling him, both of them, toward hard ground. Jerking her flush against his body, he twisted sharply so that *he* would be the one to make first contact with the unforgiving mountain.

The blow knocked the breath out of his lungs. The blunt hammering pain ricocheting through his body blinded him. Still Dunndrogo's instincts continued functioning as quickly as ever.

He wrapped his body around hers as best as he could. An instant later when the momentum changed, he rolled them the rest of the way downhill like a mighty felled tree.

They came to a stop a few yards inside the woods, where the encroaching sunset had already yielded to dusk. The first thing Dunndrogo noticed was that the world had changed from green and amber, to muted shades of gray. The second thing he grew aware of was the feel of Paloma gasping for breath and trembling beneath him.

She was alive. As he drew her scent deep into his lungs, he knew that no matter how upset she might be with him, *that* was all that mattered. Alive.

"Let me go," she half cried and half gasped.

"No. Not yet. You sweet fool, don't you realize you could have killed yourself just now? What of your precious animals then? What would have become of them?"

"I wasn't... I didn't... Oh, God, I wish I could hate you!"

He closed his eyes, but there could be no protecting himself from it. Their unique connection made her pain his, and vice versa. Neither of them could escape the other's passion or torment.

"Paloma, listen to me. I didn't regret last night," he ground out against her ear. His voice was no steadier than hers.

"Then why are you talking about leaving?"

"Because it was more than I ever dreamed I could have," he rasped. "Because it's more than I had a right to take. When I watched you with my mother this morning it struck me that I'll never fit in your world. Never."

"You didn't take anything I wasn't prepared to give."

Her provocative words had an immediate, inevitable affect, and he felt himself swell and harden against her. The urge to take what he desperately wanted, to rip her thin T-shirt and jeans from her and truly sate himself in her pure body was almost uncontrollable. With an oath, Dunndrogo fought the demons inside him, but he couldn't resist burying his face more deeply into her lush hair.

"It can't be enough for you," he rasped. "*I* can't be enough for you."

"Don't say that! Being with you was, *is* everything I could ever want. How many times am I going to have to prove that to you before you'll believe me?"

As she spoke she turned her head and tried to press her lips to his jaw, to the corner of his mouth. It was a sweet agony from which he couldn't bring himself to pull away. But he knew he had to make her see reason.

"Paloma, I beg you," he moaned, twisting his head away.

"No, I'm begging *you*. Dunndrogo, don't you realize that when I look into your eyes, I see the missing part of my own soul? I feel as though I've been searching for you all my life! I can't bear to think of a world without you."

He stopped fighting.

Slowly, he lowered his head to rest beside hers again. "Sweet angel," he whispered.

"Don't leave me, Dunndrogo. I would die. You know I would."

And he would, too. The knowledge of that, and of knowing she deserved the chance at a more normal life, made him feel as though he was being pulled apart, inch by inch. "I want so much more for you."

"I have all I want. Don't reject me. Make love to me. Really make love to me. I'm not afraid."

With a groan he yielded to the need to press his lower body harder against hers. Once. Twice. Hunger for her ached in him so. Still, he couldn't risk letting himself lose control, and he fought not to take what she'd offered so generously.

But he wanted to. Oh, how he wanted to.

Only he knew she could never survive it.

Paloma, all the demons in hell won't tempt me to destroy your precious body with mine. I hold it, I hold you, too dear.

But you're in pain. We both are.

Then take me into your mind again, my heart. It's the only safe way. Dream with me, and I'll share my beast's passion with you for as long as you can bear me.

No, for as long as you want me.

Dunndrogo groaned, and as gently as possible let himself nip at her shoulder. *I'll want you beyond the grave. Haven't you realized that by now?*

The combination of his caress and his intense vow won a beguiling whimper from Paloma. *What do you want me to do?*

Just open to me . . . and let me love you.

He raised himself on his forearms, and with not-quite-steady fingers brushed her hair away from her face. The tender smile of trust she gave him was like a vise around his heart.

Closing his eyes, he set the scene this time, picturing her rising out of his secret pool, dressed in nothing more than moonlight. He stepped out of the shadows and when she saw him, her welcoming smile was as lovely as the one she'd just awarded him.

She took his breath away. With worshipping hands, he caressed the delicate swell of her breasts, then bent to the tempting pink nipples that the cool water and desire had beaded into taut points.

Paloma sighed and used his shoulders to keep herself upright. The sensations that swept through her body echoed those charging through his, so that when he coaxed her to turn around, she shifted with eagerness, allowing him not only the continued privilege of caressing and exploring her exquisite body, but also to align her more satisfyingly against his fiercely aroused flesh.

As her breath gushed out of her, she rocked her head back against his chest and covered his hands with her own. Dunndrogo watched her from beneath passion-heavy lids.

Yes, that's beautiful... so beautiful.

Dunndrogo, I ache.

Show me where.

Although he could squeeze the life out of another being with one hand, he found the patience, the tenderness to let her slender fingers lead him on an inch-by-inch journey over alabaster, sleek skin to the raven-black curls that were softer than silk.

Here?

Yes.

Here?

He ventured farther, until he found moist satin. Ever so carefully, he tested her sensitivity and readiness for him, not at all surprised when she cried out and spasmodically gripped his wrist to intensify the contact.

I can't wait to bury myself there. You're so small, so hot, so moist. All night I dreamed of how it felt to have you wrapped around me. I could hear your breath grow shallow as it is now, and your voice break when I touched you here.

As before, she responded when he located the fragile, vulnerable heart of her. To intensify the sensation, he brushed her hair aside and leaned over to spread a series of impassioned kisses down the length of her neck and across her shoulder. His need until then was only to prove to her how glorious and desirable she was to him.

But when she reached back to link her arms around his neck, the inviting arch of her body, and the nearness of her lips ignited newer, stronger fires of recklessness within him. Knowing he was edging toward a danger point, but unable to resist one of the ancient instincts burning within him, he drew her down to the cool, damp grass so that they were both kneeling.

He spread kisses from shoulder to shoulder, and then moved aside the sweep of her hair to lightly test his teeth at her nape. All the while his hands performed their own restless exploration, cupping and caressing her breasts, coursing a trail downward to her inner thighs and back again. Finally, when he had her relaxed and leaning forward in the position that to him was as natural as it was foreign to her, he whispered in her ear.

Are you afraid?

I don't think so.

I'd rather die than hurt you, but I need—

It's all right. Do it.

Even so, he took care easing into her, aware of the power of the mind, and how she could easily feel tender from last night. But it was difficult to control the feral calls that taunted him like ghosts in the shadows—only worse because they were inside him.

They called to him to abandon control, to take what he wanted, to claim his own fierce satisfaction. So powerful were the voices, he realized too late that his hands were biting into her small waist and leaving marks.

Don't stop! You're not hurting me!

Despite her entreaty, he'd been deeply jarred, and for an instant Dunndrogo froze, not sure whether to believe her words were a gift or the truth. Reality or fantasy. He was only beginning to understand the wonder of her limitless generosity. Could he trust that his beloved dream, his small woods sprite wouldn't cross the boundaries of safety, wouldn't give herself to him thereby risking everything? Did he dare take what she offered, *all* she offered, without destroying the life he cherished more than his own?

As she rose to her knees and reached back for him, he felt the power of ages congealing inside him.

Dunndrogo, come to me. Make me yours.

With a groan, he yielded to her entreaty and his desire. But not the voices. Never the voices, he promised himself. He rejected them as completely as he claimed her.

"Paloma," he whispered, her presence around him both soothing and provocative. "Your love frees me. Frees me."

She brushed her cheek against the hand on her shoulder. "Show me, my dark ghost."

Lowering her back to the grass, he raced her toward ecstasy, and found his own heaven.

CHAPTER THIRTEEN

"I don't want you to go. I already miss you."

Dunndrogo's gruff admission made Paloma tremble as much as his passion had reduced her to being all throbbing sensation moments ago. Now, as darkness became a cloak all its own, he sat leaning against a great pine holding her in his arms, and the strong steady beat of his heart was a symphony she didn't want to end.

"You know I'm with you no matter where either of us is," she replied, feeling an unusually strong need to reassure him. Because of what they'd just shared, or a result of his behavior earlier at the estate? She was too tired, too sated to think.

"Yes...and my mother will be concerned about you. You'll find she's very good at worrying. That's how she hurt herself in the first place."

"Old Harry will fuss, too, if I don't get back, and so will the girls."

He made a sound deep in his chest that might have been a laugh, if Dunndrogo was the type for laughter. "Stolen moments," he murmured, pressing a kiss to the crown of her head. It ended in a sigh. "What are we going to do, my heart?"

"Is a decision written in stone necessary?"

"You've given me your mind, your heart, and in a very special way, your body. We're linked more deeply than people who stand in a church and take vows, yet I can't forget that I'm cheating you from a normal life."

Paloma sat up. "*Isaac Tredway* is cheating us from a normal life. The important thing is that we're fooling him. We're proving we can make our own happiness despite everything."

He studied her in silence for a long moment before carefully touching her cheek. "Despite everything. You'll have to tolerate my doubts, Paloma. There's something in the air tonight."

How odd. She felt a difference, too. "Trouble?" she asked, immediately more alert.

"I don't know. But it's not our imagination. I sense it in the creatures hovering in the shadows, as well."

"Perhaps there's another storm coming." She checked the sky that had begun to twinkle with stars.

"I don't think so, but if there is one, I'm glad my mother is at the compound with you."

"And I'd better get back before Old Harry convinces her to let him out to look for me. He can be irresistibly persuasive when he sets his mind to it."

"I'll walk you back."

Paloma only let him go part of the way. Despite his keen eyesight, she didn't want him out in the darkness, especially near the road, anymore than he wanted her there. Just as they reached the wider path that led directly to the compound, she stopped him, gently placing her hand to his chest.

"I'll be fine from here."

"There's barely any light coming from the compound. Let me take you the rest of the way."

"There's enough. I lit the lamps for Maeve before I left. Besides, I could find my way back there with my eyes closed, especially if Daisy and Old Harry are in a chatty or argumentative mood," she added with a smile, as she thought of how noisy those two could get.

"Are you sure?"

"You worry too much."

He looked away. "You're my treasure, how can I not?"

Realizing she'd hurt and upset him with her attempt at flippancy, Paloma quickly wrapped her arms around him and pressed her cheek to his chest. "Oh, God . . . I'm sorry. I'm only trying to reassure you because you seem so unhappy now."

"Perhaps it's a lingering emotion that has something to do with what the French call 'the little death.'"

The subtle teasing was a lovely surprise for her, and she smiled dreamily as she traced the rawhide tie of his tunic. "I think you've been reading more entertaining books than I have." Glancing up at him from beneath her lashes, she added, "Let's not let our fears defeat us, Dunndrogo. You made me soar tonight. I'm still feeling it. I want to carry your taste and the memory of your touch with me throughout the night. Not fear."

He made a sound of surprise—or dismay?—and crushed her so close, she could feel the mighty beat of his heart. "Even your thoughts are beautiful. Then sweet dreams, my own."

"They will be because you'll be in them."

Rising quickly on tiptoe, she kissed him. Smiling at his rapt expression, she ran off toward the estate.

She'd meant what she'd said, she could have floated for the euphoria she was feeling. Despite the undercurrents, the darkness seemed to caress her tonight. And yet the closer she got to the house, the more she realized Dunndrogo had been right, there was also a strange aura in the woods. An unsettledness.

Yards away from the opened iron gates, she found the reason why. She hadn't left the gates open, as they were now. Breaking into a panicked sprint, she raced the rest of the way, and in the glow of the lantern someone had placed out on the porch, she spotted a familiar vehicle.

She almost groaned in relief. Byron, the only other person with a key to the front gates, had surprised them with a visit. It was only Thursday, and admittedly that gave her some doubts, until she recalled how when she'd stayed at the farm, he'd occasionally visited during the week. If he'd been working too hard and decided he'd needed a break. If he'd gotten spooked and had wanted to check on her...

But she became uneasy again when she remembered Maeve. Would Dunndrogo's mother have panicked at his arrival? Foolish question; of course, she would. *That's* probably what she and Dunndrogo had been feeling.

As she hurried for the house, the front door swung open and Byron came rushing out. Paloma waved.

"Hello!" she began. "It's wonderful to—"

"Where the heck have you been? And who's the woman in there? She won't tell me a thing. She practically held me at bay with the point of Old Harry's umbrella."

"She's...a new friend," Paloma said cautiously. "If you'd introduced yourself, you would know that."

"Paloma. Cut the games. Tredway's coming."

"*What?*"

"We've no time to waste, and you have to come clean with me. That woman in there looks like something out of a different century, and I have a feeling she didn't stop by on her way to a costume ball, either. What's more, Daisy's been doing some pretty bizarre pantomiming, and you're prowling the woods at night. What's going on here?" Byron demanded again, clenching her right wrist.

Paloma eased herself free. It wasn't that Byron's grip hurt or upset her, but it simply seemed wrong to have his touch obliterating the memory of Dunndrogo's. "That will have to wait, Byron. Tell me what you know about Isaac. How do you know he's coming?"

The young scientist raked his hair back off his forehead. Assuming a hands-on-hips stance, he snapped, "The dim-witted temporary receptionist at our offices finally got around to telling me this afternoon about a call she took yesterday evening just before she left for the day. It was a man. He asked questions. Questions she had no answers to, but that I was able to link to another study you and I collaborated on, which I later merged into my own research. The caller then tried another approach and mentioned having tried to contact me over the weekend. That's when she helpfully informed him that I'd been on a trip to see friends in *west* Maine.''

"No. Oh, God, how did she know?"

"Would you believe she confessed she has a thing for me? Out of curiosity she'd asked one of my co-workers, and that's the story I always give him when I'm going to be out of reach. Damn," he muttered. "And I was so careful giving out information."

"Never mind," Paloma said, compassionately touching his arm. She glanced around, trying not to let panic gain too much control. "The important thing is to figure out how much time we have."

"Zero. Hell, honey, you're just lucky he didn't show up last night. But I phoned the university as soon as I got that news, and I was told Dr. Tredway left the university early this afternoon after giving a special seminar."

"Then there's no time to lose," Paloma whispered. Her head started reeling from the horrible scenarios her imagination began to spin. She pointed to his truck. "Turn that around, and bring my vehicle up front. The keys are in it. I'll go inside and get everyone ready to leave."

Secretly she tried to warn Dunndrogo, but either her anxiety was interfering, or he was too preoccupied himself. Whatever the case, she couldn't feel the usual chemistry that told her they were connecting.

"Paloma! Thank heavens," Maeve cried, as she entered the house. The older woman was struggling to balance herself on a broken mop stick. She wore a blanket over her nightgown like a shawl, and looked every bit the eccentric that Byron had said. "What's happening? I wouldn't tell that young man a thing. Why is he so upset?"

"He's a friend, Maeve. He saved our lives before. You can trust him. But he brought bad news. Isaac Tredway is coming. We have to get away. Now."

"Dear God. I have to get back to the cave and warn Dunndrogo."

"There's no time. I've even tried to send him messages, but I'm not feeling him. You have to come with us. The best thing we can do for him would be to lead Isaac away from the woods, and especially not let him know about the cave or Dunndrogo."

"Yes. Yes, you're right. Where will we go?"

"I haven't the foggiest notion. The most important thing at the moment is to not get trapped here."

Together the women soothed understandably upset Old Harry and the chimps, and after Paloma grabbed her journals, they hurried outside.

Byron had maneuvered both cars up front. The idling engines seemed unusually loud, and their combined headlights created an eerie bright light. Paloma thought that even if he couldn't hear the engines, Dunndrogo might have spotted the lights. If he'd been on his way back up the mountain.

Dunndrogo, if you can feel me, be careful. There's danger. Stay away and I'll contact you as soon as I can. I love you.

Forcing herself to ignore the burning in her eyes, she turned to his mother. "Maeve, you and the others climb into the van, and I'll— Where's Byron?"

She'd been looking around for him and realized he was nowhere to be seen. The fine hairs on her arms lifted.

"Get in. Quickly," she said to her group. Her stomach clenching into a more aching knot, she began circling the van. Just as she came between the two vehicles, she saw the sprawled legs. "Byron!" she gasped, recognizing his shoes and jeans.

Was he unconscious? Dead? Paloma backed away from the scene, a new terror gripping her.

"Oh, don't disappoint me by running away, my dear. Not yet, at any rate. After all, we haven't celebrated our reunion yet."

Paloma didn't need to see him to recognize the voice. It was one that underscored every nightmare, and had threatened every hour of every waking day since she'd escaped from his laboratory.

Isaac Tredway rose from behind the cover of her vehicle.

Even as she backed up toward Maeve and the animals, she heard their gasps and whimpers as they spotted him, too. She hoped that Maeve would stay silent, and that the animals wouldn't panic, either. There was always a chance, especially since this was not the Isaac Tredway she remembered.

Something had happened, she thought as he inched around her vehicle.

"My apologies for being tardy," he said almost pleasantly. "I had a minor accident on my way here."

He looked terrible. Besides the pronounced limp, and a shoulder he was favoring, he was soaking wet, from thinning salt-and-pepper hair, to his outdated gray suit, to muddy suede loafers.

"Don't let my humbled appearance deceive you," he added, drolly. Pausing to lean against her right headlight, he lifted the gun in his right hand and aimed it at her. "I can still pull a trigger."

"What happened?" Paloma asked, inching another step back and away from the van.

"That damned dirt road leading past the lake. It's barely wide enough for one car even when the brush is trimmed back. Something darted in front of me and I overcompensated. Drove off the bank and into the water. Fortunately, I have a selection of replacements to choose from, eh?"

Paloma thought of the animal that had spooked her near that same area. "It's too bad you didn't hit your head," she offered coldly. "It might have knocked some sense into you. This isn't going to work, Isaac. No matter what you're planning."

"But I've been looking forward to this moment for a long time, lovely Paloma. And, I think if I have one of your precious little apes in my car as a hostage, you'd sound a great deal more respectful and agreeable than you do now. So, why don't you choose one of the females, the more docile one, I think, and bring her out here."

"You'll have to shoot me first," Paloma replied, taking another step in the opposite direction. If she could draw his attention long enough, perhaps she could mentally coax Old Harry to escape and take the girls with him.

"Ah, well, you know I don't want to do that," Isaac replied, his smile sardonic. "After all, I have such plans for you. But..." he advanced a bit more and peered into the open van "...I think your elderly companion would understand the need for sacrifice, wouldn't you, old girl?"

"You'd better do a good job with the first bullet, you bastard," Maeve shot back. "Because I've been waiting thirty years for the opportunity to repay you."

Intrigued, Isaac shuffled closer and squinted into the vehicle. "I know that voice. Who are... My word. Maeve Cooper, it is you. A miracle, I'd say—if I believed in them."

"I do," Paloma said, moving again. She knew she had a greater responsibility now. She had to keep Maeve alive, as well.

Isaac chuckled and waved his automatic. "This is actually becoming more enjoyable than I'd thought. I should have guessed you would end up here, Paloma, knowing you're aware of how much I always loathed it. The question is, how did you, Maeve?"

Before she could answer, a feral roar filled the woods.

Paloma's breath caught in her throat. Her gaze locked with Maeve's and the older woman smiled.

"You'll find out soon enough."

Although he'd looked momentarily startled at the howl, he recovered and nodded. "Properly cryptic, and impressively atmospheric, whatever that was out there. I'm entertained. Perhaps I'll spare you after all, just for the pleasure of finding out what you've been up to. I'm beginning to recall that you were to be my first human subject, but you slipped out of my clutches." He backed away a bit to bring Paloma into his view. "Congratulations, my pet, at least my property doesn't look worse for wear. If you please, load the female in her cage and put her in Dr. Metcalf's car."

"I don't own any cages."

He looked momentarily stunned. Then he threw back his head and laughed. "Good grief, you're serious," he added when he discovered she hadn't so much as blinked. "You've actually tried to befriend these beasts?"

"They're not going back with you," she asserted, ignoring the foolish question. Secretly her mind was racing. Where was Dunndrogo? That he'd signaled to them filled her with hope, but fear for him.

"That sounds like a threat. Have you forgotten what I can do to bad little girls when they've misbehaved?"

Memories of the darkness, of terrible sounds and bad smells came alive in Paloma's mind, and she took an involuntary step back.

"Paloma," Maeve murmured. "It's time. Call Dunndrogo."

Aghast, she stared. "No!"

"Who's Dunndrogo?" Isaac asked, glancing from one to the other.

As Maeve opened her mouth to answer, Old Harry began to pantomime. Paloma stepped forward. *Harry, stop, Hair say. Make danger for Ghost. Must wait.*

He did stop, but his gaze was melancholy and frightened. Isaac didn't miss it. "What did you just do with him? Well,'' he murmured, looking suddenly satisfied. "So I was right, that was your research I read about in young Metcalf's article. Interesting. I can see we're going to have a lot to talk about once I get you back to the laboratory."

"I told you, we're not going. Ever."

"But I have a need for my specimens, Paloma. And especially you. You'll make a fine mother. Oh, your build is a bit too small, but your capacity to communicate with the beasts is rather impressive. A handy little thing to have around to keep down riots. I'll just have to remember to take your young before they're fully developed, won't I?"

Feeling sick to her stomach, Paloma knew if he hadn't been before, Isaac was totally mad now. Their only chance was to fight for time, and pray Dunndrogo *could* save them.

"Why, Uncle Isaac?" she whispered, purposely sounding heartbroken and confused. "Why all these bizarre experiments, the sacrificed animals? What have you proved after all these years except your skill at cruelty and mutilation?"

He looked thoroughly astonished. "I'm not a cruel man. I'm a man of vision. I'm carrying science forward to the day when there'll be a new order of man. Disease-resistant, intellectually incomparable and possessing superhuman strength. I'll be famous. The world will revere me. And I think I'm close, Paloma. I just need my papers." He blinked as though coming out of a trance and leveled the gun at her again. "You have my papers, don't you?"

Daisy and Ditto started to wail. Old Harry shuddered and flung himself at his former jailer. Unfortunately, Isaac's instincts were still reliable and he'd begun to alter his aim. Seeing tragedy in slow motion, Paloma launched herself forward.

"No!" she cried.

The gun discharged. Luckily, she'd ruined Isaac's aim enough to protect Harry, but when the crazed man tried to jerk free, his gun struck the orangutan and sent him sprawling back into the van.

That left Paloma, and she was no match for someone out of control, even if he was injured. Isaac had always prided himself on keeping physically fit—it was part of his fascination with perfecting the species—and it paid off as she tried to wrestle the gun from him.

With a single blow, he knocked her to the ground, and as the world came back into focus, Paloma found herself looking up into the bore of the automatic.

Suddenly another roar filled the night. Isaac made a full turn—understandable since the earsplitting eruption of rage seemed to come from everywhere.

"What in the world?"

"I believe you're about to meet my son," Maeve announced with great satisfaction.

Confused, Isaac shook his head.

"The child I was carrying when you slipped that serum into my tea. You must have always wondered what became of us. Well, you're about to discover the result of your cruelty and madness."

As a huge shadow began striding toward them from the darkness, fear registered on Isaac's face. He stooped to jerk Paloma up off the ground. He placed her before him like a shield.

"Is that what you would call an 'acceptable mutation,' as I believe you used to call it, *Doctor?*" Maeve asked coldly.

Paloma saw her chance. She grabbed Isaac's gun hand and slammed it into the side of her van. He cried out in pain, and the gun went flying.

He swung out at her with his injured arm, only knocking her off balance, but in that instant Dunndrogo attacked.

This, Paloma realized as she watched in dreaded fascination, was what Dunndrogo had warned her about all along, as had Maeve. He was no longer the tragic, achingly tender lover she'd lost her heart to. Consumed by the wildness within him, he used his claws and with one sweep across Isaac Tredway's throat, stole his voice forever. With another, he lacerated the scientist's suit and shirt.

Paloma averted her face as Isaac's white shirt turned red. That's when she saw Byron. Still dazed, he was struggling to crawl for the gun, while staring horrified at Dunndrogo.

She darted over to him and grappled with him for it. "No, Byron!"

"For the love of heaven, Paloma, let go before it kills all of us!"

"You don't understand—he's saved our lives!"

In the ensuing silence Byron stared at her, to Dunndrogo, and then back at her. She saw the disbelief in his eyes, and the curiosity. But her concern was for Dunndrogo. As he backed off the corpse, he looked at what he'd done and bowed his head.

Paloma's heart ached for what she knew he was feeling. There was satisfaction in knowing that he'd finally achieved retribution for the tragedy inflicted on his mother. But at the same time he'd been forced to humiliate himself before the people he cared about.

To her amazement, Old Harry reacted first. As she was handing the gun to Maeve to hold, the orangutan slipped out of the van and went to Dunndrogo. With unmistakable compassion, he placed a hand on his back.

Good Ghost kill Monster dead.

Paloma gasped. Then she crossed determinedly over to Dunndrogo herself.

As she approached him, he averted his face.

"No," she murmured, reaching up to turn him back to her.

"I'd have given anything to spare you having to witness that," he said bitterly. "But when I saw him hurt you..."

"I'm all right," she whispered, stroking his face with the backs of her fingers. "We're all all right."

"Yes, except that now you know what I really am."

"You're the kindest, bravest soul on the face of this earth," she replied firmly.

Staring at her as though he couldn't believe what she was saying, he suddenly uttered a feral groan and swept her into his arms and buried his face in the thick fall of her hair.

She could feel him trembling as he struggled to regain control. Maybe she was trembling, too. She wasn't sure. All she knew was that she was where she wanted to stay. Forever.

"My God," Byron whispered, behind them. "Paloma?"

Reluctantly, she eased back to meet her friend's shocked gaze. Poor Byron, she thought. She didn't know how he was going to reconcile this in his mind, and she could already see that he was hurt because of the telling way she and Dunndrogo were embracing and looking at one another.

"Byron," she began gently, "I'd like you to meet Dunndrogo."

Her friend rubbed at his face with both hands. "Uh-huh. Paloma, we need to talk."

Wincing because he hadn't really acknowledged Dunndrogo, she touched Dunndrogo's chest in a silent plea for patience and went to Byron. "I'm so sorry," she murmured, understanding his disappointment in her.

He managed a lopsided smile. Barely. "Heck, sweetheart, I should have figured it out. I always knew the guy who won your heart was going to have to be a pretty rare person. But," he added, glancing around her at Dunndrogo, "how was I supposed to know you were going to pick something straight out of a fairy tale?"

"He is very special, Byron."

"Honey, he's a wild man."

"He possesses the most beautiful soul, and that's all I see, Byron."

"And how are you going to explain that beautiful soul to the police? Because they *will* come, you know."

CHAPTER FOURTEEN

The sheriff's department began arriving shortly after noon the next day after it had been reported by two youngsters fishing at the town lake that the tail end of a car could be seen jutting out of the water. A file check on the New Jersey license plates revealed that the vehicle belonged to one Dr. Isaac Tredway, and the search was on.

Sheriff Ian McMann had been with the initial party to appear at the front gates, and he'd explained to Paloma with grandfatherly compassion that there was a good possibility her guardian had suffered a heart attack as he'd driven to visit her, and that the body in all probability would never be found.

"'Course, the dogs did pick up a scent near where the car went in, so it's not impossible that Dr. Tredway survived the crash, only to get himself lost out in these woods. We'll put the dogs out and do our best to find him, Ms. St. John."

For the next two days, both Paloma and Maeve held their breath as deputies were called in along with game warden officials, and an all-out search commenced.

Explaining her relationship with Isaac had been a tricky situation for Paloma. So was creating a story to establish Maeve's presence at the compound. They created a history that wasn't so far off from the truth—as it would have been, had Isaac not played God with so many lives.

It was the dogs that remained their chief concern. Hour after hour they listened to the barking and yapping in the woods, praying all the while that Dunndrogo remained safe and undiscovered. They literally wept from relief when it finally rained heavily the first night of the search.

Late on the second day, the sheriff called off the investigation. "I'm sorry, ladies," the stocky law official said, trying to look sympathetic, when it was obvious he felt dirty, tired and ready for a shower and a long nap. "That storm just about shut down all our hopes. Then this morning the dogs picked up some scent that scared the heck out of them, and they've been useless ever since. That's the other reason I'm here.

"You ladies are familiar with the stories of something roaming these woods? Well, from the behavior of those dogs, it's a good guess that it's still out there. Could be Dr. Tredway ran smack into it. I apologize for being indelicate about the matter, but it's best you know what you're up against. I don't think we're ever going to find a body."

It hadn't been difficult for Paloma or Maeve to appear aggrieved; after all, they each stored a lifetime's supplies of heartbreaking memories to keep them pale and reticent. In the end Paloma had thanked Sheriff McMann, explaining that while she and her uncle hadn't spoken much over the past year or so because of their differing philosophies regarding the study of animals, she would prefer to believe he'd been driving out to make peace. "That's probably the best attitude to take, Ms. St. John," the sheriff replied, awkwardly patting her shoulder. "And, again, I apologize for my bluntness before. The only reason I'm not protecting you from anything is because I'd like to impress on the two of you how dangerous it is out beyond those walls. It would rest my mind a great deal if you two would consider moving into town. There's plenty of land available where you could raise your animals without any interference."

Paloma thanked him, but told him they were happy and at peace here in the compound. "By the way," she'd added, as she walked him to the front gates, "do you know a young man by the name of Douglas Westman?"

When the sheriff acknowledged he did, she told him about meeting him in the woods a while back, and about his lost pet. The sheriff's barrel chest shook with quiet laughter. "That fool animal trotted back into the Westman's front yard a few days later. Mrs. Westman got up to make coffee one morning and found it eating her bedding plants and took a broom to it. Folks say you could hear her hollering for a mile."

"Well, you see then," Paloma replied, glad for the animal, and determined to use it for their benefit, "if a goat rambled through the woods without any harm coming to it, then surely we're fine behind these walls?"

Shaking his head, the older man told her he certainly hoped so, and soon took his leave.

Back in the house, Paloma filled Maeve in on the rest of the sheriff's comments, as the two settled down by the kitchen table to unwind with a cup of tea.

"Do you think it's over?" Maeve asked, her expression indicating that she was still afraid to hope.

"Yes. At least that part. Remember Sheriff McCann said that the authorities in New Jersey reported their inspection of Isaac's home proved disconcerting because of some other journals they'd found down in his laboratory, not to mention the specimens he kept. Those journals must be new projects he was beginning to work on, or else he was trying to redraft from memory the ones I took."

"I'm glad he'll be found out for being the true monster he was."

"I doubt he will be, Maeve. The university will do its best to downplay that if they can. The important thing will be to discover who'll get possession of all that research."

"Do you know if he had a will?" Maeve asked.

Paloma shook her head. "I rather doubt it. Isaac's philosphies lead me to believe he was the type who didn't worry about such things because he thought he would live forever."

"Good. That means, as his only legal living heir, it will probably be you."

Paloma shuddered. "I don't want anything of his."

"No, of course not," Maeve agreed. "But it would be an ironic justice if in the end Isaac's fortune was used to counteract everything he'd worked to destroy."

"The important thing is that Dunndrogo will be safer now," Paloma said, reaching across the table to cover the woman's hand with hers. "We'll all be safer."

Paloma waited another hour to make sure the authorities had, indeed, left the area, before setting out for the cave. She could barely contain her excitement. As it was, she ran the last quarter mile, and climbed the mountain to the cave at a near sprint.

Breathless, she ran straight into Dunndrogo just inside the mouth of the cave. He crushed her close as though it had been weeks since they'd been together rather than days.

"I felt you coming to me," he rasped, alternately caressing her hair and face, and planting kisses there. "It was all I could do not to race down and meet you."

"I know. I felt you every bit as much as you did me. Oh, Dunndrogo, I've missed you so."

"Every minute has been a torture."

They needed several quiet moments to just stand there in each other's arms to assure themselves that they were indeed together again. Finally, Dunndrogo sighed and put her at arm's length to gaze at her solemnly. "So... is it over?"

"The worst part, I think."

She filled him in on everything that had transpired. Throughout her story, he listened, his expression grave. He nodded frequently, injecting a question when he needed more clarification. In the end he, too, seemed satisfied.

"I think Mother is right. They'll award you his estate."

"If they do, I'll take great pleasure in burning his work."

"It will mean you'll have to go away for a while." His magnificent face already showed the stress she knew he tried to keep out of his voice.

"Not for long," she assured him. Then she grew somber. "Dunndrogo—what did you do with the body?"

A satisfied look came into his eyes. "Come, I'll show you," he said, and led her down the path into the cave.

He took her straight through to the inner cavern, down the narrow, treacherous path where the low thunder built to an ominous roar.

Paloma was awed by the darkly fascinating place. Because of the noise level, she spoke to Dunndrogo telepathically.

I understand your fascination with this cavern. It vibrates with life, as you do.

This is where I came to think of you.

And Isaac?

Dunndrogo pointed to the black space beyond the edge of the falls. Together they stood and watched the mist rise from the belly of the earth like so many spirits.

It's both beautiful and terrifying.

Yes. Perhaps the doctor has found the hell he deserves.

Dunndrogo's thought made Paloma nod. There was great power and final judgment here. It seemed fitting that Isaac should end up where he would appear his most insignificant.

Wanting to get Dunndrogo's mind off the man who'd brought him so much pain, she drew him back up the path and out into the warmth of the setting sun, although they were careful to stay hidden by the wall.

Paloma told him of her plans to call Byron in the morning.

At the mention of him, Dunndrogo grew somber.

"What is it? What's wrong?"

"He's a good man, Paloma. He proved it by what he risked trying to warn you. And I can't forget what he said to you the other night. He's right about me, and the feelings he holds for you... I think he could make you happy if you gave him a chance."

"Do you think I could turn my back on what we have?" Paloma whispered, aghast.

"He could give you children. Paloma, you have such a capacity for love. It should be shared."

"The animals are my children. And if the day comes that I find more that need homes and compassion, then I'll take them in, too. Dunndrogo," she said, her voice breaking, "it's *you* that I love. Don't you know that by now?"

With a groan, he drew her quickly, desperately into his arms. "Yes. *Yes.* But up until now, I haven't let myself think of it as mine to possess and cherish. I haven't let myself hope to believe it could last. I still can't get over how this could be. That's why I had to give you the freedom to choose. But...Paloma, I love you, with all my heart, and soul. I will until my final breath and beyond."

Her own heart overflowing with love, Paloma pressed her cheek to his. "It will be good," she whispered. "We'll be happy."

"We'll make our happiness."

She smiled up at him. "Yes. That reminds me of something else I wanted to talk to you about. I've been thinking. Maeve can't keep living up here stranded and subjected to the harsh winters. I'd like to ask her to move into the house with me. She's already showing a wonderful acumen for working with the animals, and you know we're getting along much better than we did at first."

Dunndrogo nodded. "You don't know how relieved I am to hear you suggest that. It would take a great burden off my mind, and while I'm not sure she would ever admit it, I think she misses having the company of another woman around. To have one who is not only generous of heart, but understands her so well will be a source of great joy for her, I'm sure."

"Thank you." Paloma gazed up at him yearningly. "You know, you could come, too."

He shook his head and, although he stroked her hair, a shadow of an old grief darkened his eyes. "I must stay here. There will always be times when I must be alone, when you must let me be alone for both our sakes. It's enough, more than enough to know that I always have your love with me."

"Always," Paloma said fervently, knowing he was right. As much as she would always believe he would never hurt her, she had to respect that he knew a part of him would always be dangerous and uncontrollable. Still, who knew...given time, and their love, anything was possible. "Always," she whispered again.

He slipped his hand under her chin and lifted her face to meet his impassioned look. "And if I call you to me, my lady, my dream?" he murmured, desire flaring unmistakably in his beautiful eyes.

Paloma reached up to touch the mysterious face so very dear to her. "Then I will come. Whenever you want me. However you want me."

Murmuring something inaudible, Dunndrogo grasped her hand and pressed a passionate kiss into her palm. Then he drew her close to his heart and gazed up at the brilliantly golden-orange sky. "Then I am the most blessed of God's creatures."

"We both are," Paloma amended, her heart at peace.

And, as the sun descended and dusk cocooned them in its protective shroud, for the first time, Paloma felt him actually believe.

*   *   *   *   *

He staked his claim…

HONOR BOUND

by
New York Times
Bestselling Author

previously published under the pseudonym Erin St. Claire

As Aislinn Andrews opened her mouth to scream, a hard
hand clamped over her face and she found herself face-
to-face with Lucas Greywolf, a lean, lethal-looking
Navajo and escaped convict who swore he wouldn't hurt
her— *if* she helped him.

Look for HONOR BOUND at your favorite
retail outlet this January.

Only from…

Silhouette

where passion lives.   SBHB

Take 4 bestselling love stories FREE

Plus get a FREE surprise gift!

Relive the romance...
Harlequin and Silhouette
are proud to present

ℬ𝓎 𝓡𝑒𝓆𝓊𝑒𝓈𝓉™

A program of collections of three complete novels by the most requested
authors with the most requested themes. Be sure to look for one volume each
month with three complete novels by top name authors.

In January: **WESTERN LOVING**   Susan Fox
                                    JoAnn Ross
                                    Barbara Kaye

Loving a cowboy is easy—taming him isn't!

In February: **LOVER, COME BACK!**   Diana Palmer
                                        Lisa Jackson
                                        Patricia Gardner Evans

It was over so long ago—yet now they're calling, "Lover, Come Back!"

In March: **TEMPERATURE RISING**   JoAnn Ross
                                      Tess Gerritsen
                                      Jacqueline Diamond

Falling in love—just what the doctor ordered!

Available at your favorite retail outlet.

REQ-G3

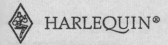

HARLEQUIN®   Silhouette

When the only time you have for yourself is...

Christmas is such a busy time—with shopping, decorating, writing cards, trimming trees, wrapping gifts....

When you do have a few *stolen moments* to call your own, treat yoursel to a brand-new *short* novel. Relax with one of our Stocking Stuffers—or with all six!

Each STOLEN MOMENTS title
is a complete and original contemporary romance that's the perfect length for the busy woman of the nineties! Especially at Christmas...

And they make perfect **stocking stuffers**, too! (For your mother, grandmother, daughters, friends, co-workers, neighbors, aunts, cousins—all the other women in your life!)

Look for the STOLEN MOMENTS display in December

STOCKING STUFFERS:

HIS MISTRESS Carrie Alexander
DANIEL'S DECEPTION Marie DeWitt
SNOW ANGEL Isolde Evans
THE FAMILY MAN Danielle Kelly
THE LONE WOLF Ellen Rogers
MONTANA CHRISTMAS Lynn Russell

HSM:

**Silhouette Books
is proud to present
our best authors,
their best books...
and the best in
your reading pleasure!**

Throughout 1993, look for exciting
books by these top names in
contemporary romance:

DIANA PALMER—
The Australian in October

FERN MICHAELS—
Sea Gypsy in October

ELIZABETH LOWELL—
Chain Lightning in November

CATHERINE COULTER—
The Aristocrat in December

JOAN HOHL—
Texas Gold in December

LINDA HOWARD—
Tears of the Renegade in January '94

When it comes to passion,
we wrote the book. BOBT3

Fifty red-blooded, white-hot, true-blue hunks
from every State in the Union!

Look for MEN MADE IN AMERICA! Written by some
of our most poplar authors, these stories feature fifty of
the strongest, sexiest men, each from a different state in
the union!

Two titles available every other month at your favorite
retail outlet.

In January, look for:

DREAM COME TRUE by Ann Major (Florida)
WAY OF THE WILLOW by Linda Shaw (Georgia)

In March, look for:

TANGLED LIES by Anne Stuart (Hawaii)
ROGUE'S VALLEY by Kathleen Creighton (Idaho)

You won't be able to resist MEN MADE IN AMERICA!

HE'S AN

AMERICAN HERO

January 1994 rings in the New Year—and a new lineup of sensational American Heroes. You can't seem to get enough of these men, and we're proud to feature one each month, created by some of your favorite authors.

January: CUTS BOTH WAYS by Dee Holmes: Erin Kenyon hired old acquaintance Ashe Seager to investigate the crash that claimed her husband's life, only to learn old memories never die.

February: A WANTED MAN by Kathleen Creighton: Mike Lanagan's exposé on corruption earned him accolades...and the threat of death. Running for his life, he found sanctuary in the arms of Lucy Brown—but for how long?

March: COOPER by Linda Turner: Cooper Rawlings wanted nothing to do with the daughter of the man who'd shot his brother. But when someone threatened Susannah Patterson's life, he found himself riding to the rescue....

AMERICAN HEROES: Men who give all they've got for their country, their work—the women they love.

Only from

Share in the joys of finding happiness and exchanging the ultimate gift—love—in full-length classic holiday treasures by two bestselling authors

JOAN HOHL
EMILIE RICHARDS

Available in December at
your favorite retail outlet.

Only from ▼ *Silhouette*® where passion lives.